MOONSTONE INTRIGUE

MOONSTONE INTRIGUE

A Romance

by

William Maltese

Writing as "Willa Lambert"

The Borgo Press
An Imprint of Wildside Press

MMVII

SECOND EDITION

1

Melissa Jordan's black hair danced in the down draft.

"Tell me, Melissa, does your associate see me as some kind of monster?" Christian shouted above the noise of the rotors as he assisted Melissa across the storage bay of the large helicopter. "Miss Howard seemed reluctant to let me hitch this ride."

He was certainly perceptive. Elizabeth hadn't trusted Christian from the start. She felt that meteorites should be used for research not frivolously wasted on knife handles.

"First off, Mr. Wynard," Melissa shouted back, "Elizabeth Howard is hardly my 'associate,' as you well know. I'm only here because my father gave this land to Canada for a park and Elizabeth needed someone with a knowledge of the area to help her find the meteorite."

"I'm disappointed that you helped Elizabeth rather than the son of the man who once made knives with your father."

"*Your* father made knives; *my* father made handles." If he didn't see the distinction, she did. "Besides, I don't recall you on my doorstep asking for help."

The meteorite was already positioned like a fossilized egg in a nest of cushioning Styrofoam. Christian's hand remained at her elbow until she sat on the bench paralleling the far wall and strapped herself in. To her annoyance, the sensation of his touch remained when his hand was removed and he slid into place beside her. In reality she'd only known Christian Wynard since this morning, but after spending nearly a week with Elizabeth and hearing her daily caustic comments about him, she felt as if she'd known him forever.

Whatever comment she might have added was interrupted by an increase in the noise level at take-off.

The ascent of the helicopter was nearly vertical; any other way risked collision with the cloud-misted, towering trees that tightly ringed the cleared, southwest Canadian landing site. As it rose, the helicopter tipped noticeably; and as a result, Christian leaned even closer to Melissa.

She endured the additional pressure of his body. On her other side she was held securely in place by a metal bulkhead that separated her from the cockpit. The contact of his body was disconcerting, but she didn't say anything. She thought he could have displayed a bit of initial discretion and left a place vacant between them.

Despite Elizabeth's warnings, Melissa had been attracted to Christian. He had a deprecating air about him that she found amusing, and he certainly had a quick come-back for Elizabeth's not too subtle put-downs. Of course, the fact that he had military-cut black hair, a crease-like dimple, a rugged jawline, and wide-set blue eyes certainly added to his allure. She imagined that as far as women and Christian Wynard went, the line formed at the right. Which line she was certainly in no hurry to join!

To counteract her awareness of him, she concentrated on

the netted meteorite which, belted even more securely into place than either Christian or Melissa, was allowed less leeway to slide.

The unexpected placement of his hand against her arm jarred her back from all her efforts at distraction. So inexplicably electric was the pressure of his fingers, insulated as her bare skin might remain beneath the protective sleeve of her jacket, she was embarrassed by it. Luckily, her strapped-in sandwiching between Christian and the metal barrier made her automatic flinch less noticeable than it would have been under less constrictive circumstances.

Now that the helicopter was airborne within a gray soup of condensed moisture diaphaneous, mist coiled and writhed like phantom snakes turned loose for a haunting. Tendrils of chill wrapped Melissa's body and weaved into one massive and clammy shroud that suffocated with claustrophobic overtones "Like a horror movie!" he suggested loudly, pointing to the cloud matter that oozed through every crack.

"I can't hear you!" she replied. Although she thought she'd gotten the gist of it, she had to agree she'd been in situations a bit more conducive to a sense of well-being. Simultaneously she told herself that her goose bumps were the direct result of the unheated storage bay and had nothing whatsoever to do with the pressure his fingers still exerted upon her.

" 'Dee dee, dee dee; dee dee, dee dee,' " he extemporaneously mouthed the theme from *The Twilight Zone* However, Melissa's sign language, namely her pointing to her ears and shaking her head, combined with lip movements that were purposely slow enough for Christian to read, indicated his observations were lost on even so obviously a captive audience He wasn't pleased at being so disadvantaged, since he suspected Melissa was leery of him because of Elizabeth's mother-hen attitude back at the recovery site.

He still found it ludicrous that Elizabeth should see him as some kind of mentally deranged psycho. On the other hand, he had to admit that with the limited information she had to go on Elizabeth's conclusions might seem logical. Except, since she was a scientist, he'd always credited her with a bit more savvy than the average woman on the street.

Christian looked for headgear that would allow more successful communication, but there was none in sight. Surrendering to the inevitable which had once again conspired against him, he settled back to contemplate what line of attack, if any, he'd put into effect once he got Melissa back to Vancouver. While he knew circumstances should have warned him away from involvement with anyone at this particular time in his life, nonetheless, he was drawn to Melissa despite her present five-day-old, wilderness "chic." Besides, he could use her scrimshaw talents.

Safely clear of treetops, the helicopter, still in a climb, veered south and penetrated the air space above cloud cover. With the addition of sunlight, mist inside the aircraft turned luminescent. Melissa watched in rapt fascination as the last of the vapor dissolved without leaving her any warmer. Actually, she'd chilled more noticeably in the cool of this higher, more brilliantly illuminated environment than she had within the shadowy, sylvan world below.

The meteorite looked no more extraordinary than it ever had; nevertheless, there was suddenly something about it, seen in this new light, that made Melissa even more anxious to be rid of it. Maybe it had something to do with how a unique rock fragment from outer space should have looked more like a rock fragment from outer space, rather than so ordinary.

Melissa turned her full attention on Christian who had closed his eyes and didn't detect her latest, most careful scrutiny of him. How could he with his trauma-punctuated past not exhibit some outer indication of the violence that had shaped, and perceivably still might shape, his existence rather than be cloaked in an exceptionally attractive a package. Why should someone who owned an extremely successful aquaculture business suddenly turn his attention to knives?

At that moment a distinctive, dull, triple "Boom!" reached her ears to silence the rock-concert blare of raucous engine and whirring airfoils. Then came the paralyzing shudder of metal all around her and the ensuing "Whoosh!" as the helicopter, with all aboard, became deadweight and dropped out of the sky.

Its death-dive wasn't a helix, graceful, slow-moving, or otherwise: that much she realized. It was an unadulterated drop. Even as it happened, her heart in her throat, her gasps from deep in her lungs, she marveled at its duration. It seemed never-ending: a scary amusement-park ride gone into perpetual downward motion.

Melissa squeezed something in a vise-like grip which turned out to be one of Christian's large hands. She no more knew when she'd laid claim to it than she could sort out anything else from the sudden jumble in her mind.

Now was time for that long-rumored replay of life that supposedly accompanied everyone's last moments on earth, and she was surprised when it didn't come.

Were there parachutes aboard? Was that what Christian was saying? No; she mentally cataloged everything: a meteorite tied and netted down on Styrofoam, the pilot, Christian, her . . .

She became one with the cataclysmic convulsion that collapsed hard metal, erupted the floor, accordianed the walls, and collapsed the roof like so much silly putty. Her spine telescoped, and her mouth shut. Only a miracle saved her teeth and jaw from fracture.

Two of the ropes that restrained the meteorite snapped and the released rock slid down a convex mound of dented metal which suddenly rose beneath it.

Cloud vapor, scooped on the ride down, became graveyard mist that lingered within a mausoleum-like darkness.

Locked in her suffering with barely any strength, Melissa heard the sounds: a roar, once distant, now a drumroll that hurt her head; a screech of metal against rock and rock against metal; and Christian's groan, or was it her own?

"Christian?" Her concern was telepathic, because she couldn't muster the strength to speak the word.

She blinked and realized only pitch-blackness, or maybe her eyesight had been damaged in the crash. No matter; what with her remaining life figured only in minutes, maybe seconds, her eyes would be just so much superfluous baggage where she was going.

She was still riding on an unstable foundation, although renewed movement was horizontal like a kicked can, or like something bounding along a flooded gutter.

"Water!" Her voice was unrecognizable.

Water was to blame for much of the increased cold and damp. Its wetness was a slow creep, from her feet to her legs, and it progressed with each passing second; her clamminess wasn't just her ebbing life-flow.

A stream or river? Water, more cushioning than solid rock, softer than rain-saturated soil. It hadn't seemed such, but that was a possible explanation for Melissa's survival. If so, she wasn't grateful as it enveloped her more completely. It wasn't fair to come so far to drown at the end.

Events might have been engineered by a higher power to give her a second chance, but Melissa wasn't convinced. What kind of a chance was it when she was too battered to take advantage of it? Her attempt to sit up met with failure. She simply hadn't the strength, the energy, or sufficient inclination. She lay there in the dark, listened to the increased roar, and felt this leaking "boat" reverberate around her as it scraped river-submerged stones. The icy water became bearable only when its numbing blessedly relieved her of her aches and pains.

"Melissa?"

She heard him, but she couldn't believe it. It was inconceivable that both had survived.

"Melissa?"

Maybe, by some twist of fate, he lived. If so, Christian was better off taking charge of his own survival, rather than wasting his time worried about hers.

She lay there, weak and tired, and didn't say a word. If she desperately wanted to find more of her usual fighting spirit, she wasn't up to the search. Not now. Maybe later.

She shut her eyes and settled in as well as she could upon a hard-metal mattress with a cold-water blanket.

A visual replay of her life began on the backs of her closed eyelids: her red-white-and-blue tricycle; her first dog, Pat; her schoolgirl crush on Mr. Perry in fourth grade . . . Faster now: her first kiss; her high-school prom; her mother's death in a skiing accident at Snowbird . . .

Water, up to her neck, rose higher. The undefined background roar grew louder. Metal grated and further dented.

"Melissa?"

She heard him.

"Still here!" Her voice was muffled and strange. "Still alive and neck-deep in water."

"Melissa?" This time, he didn't give her a chance to confirm or deny; he was afraid he'd fantasized her voice. "Thank God! I thought you were . . ." He stopped, suspicious that "dead" might be the incantation to conjure it.

Melissa was less superstitious. "Dead." Now she didn't find death quite so enticing. "You?"

"No broken bones that I can tell."

"The pilot?"

"I've not heard him, have you?"

Three out of three were odds too great to hope for, and both knew it.

"Shall we try to get out of here?" she suggested but in truth she didn't want to move. She was concerned about the pilot, though, and with the state of the wreckage, the cockpit was obviously better reached from the outside.

"I've even got the way out. A hole over this way, albeit under the water line. I'm presuming you can swim."

"From one side of a very small pool to the other." She wasn't keen on these Canadian waters, although swimming would probably do her the favor of generating some heat.

"Think you might like to move a bit farther over this way?"

"Keep talking." She didn't want to ask if it were as dark as it seemed for fear that he'd say no.

"Did anyone ever tell you that the three freckles across the bridge of your nose cry out for a fourth to provide aesthetic balance," he obliged, "or that your warm gray eyes contradict the adjective 'icy-gray'? Care to tell me how your marvelous olive complexion managed to get so burnished despite the last five days of more-off-than-on sunshine?"

"Enough!" She didn't just mean his blarney. He'd taken advantage of her successful maneuvering of the dark and watery maze by taking hold of her waist with both hands and giving a squeeze.

"You don't think there's something to be said for the braille method of getting acquainted?" He sounded amused.

"What kind of luck puts me here with you?" Melissa's question was rhetorical, but he chose to answer it.

"We came looking for the same thing. I lost. You're giving me a lift back to Vancouver in this helicopter loaned CanTec by the U.S. Government."

"Where's this exit you used to entice me over?" She reminded herself that this man's father had been a good friend and business associate of her father. In all fairness, Melissa had possibly let her opinion of him be influenced by Elizabeth's dislike of the competition in the meteorite-recovery game.

The wreckage gave another ongoing lurch, accompanied by

trash-compactor sounds.

"Exit, *that* way." He was spurred on by the renewed activity of their damaged container. His hands on Melissa's waist pointed her in the right direction. "Under water. Straight down."

The hole found Melissa, rather than vice versa, as it sucked her through with such unexpected vehemence that she gasped ice-cold water all of the way to the other side.

Melissa was washed out from beneath the wreckage like a mechanic slid from beneath the underside of a car. She was still struggling for air as she was swept over the edge of the falls.

Her one breathless scream wasn't to warn Christian but to give response to her own sheer terror. Her pitiful sound was lost within the immensity of the falling water's bull-horn roar.

Consciousness, almost unawares, rode a warmth that miraculously thawed the iceberg she'd become. She felt infinitely old: one of the first space travelers to go into suspended animation and to be brought out of hibernation after a sleep of a few-thousand years, not quite functioning properly.

She shivered: a ripple of nerves and flesh that made her feel better; although, her headache remained.

Suddenly, there was a shadow-play on her closed lids. Its hypnotic dance included light which was welcome in a world Melissa had come to believe was forever cast in grays and blacks. However, her eyes, once open, didn't continue her initial enthusiasm.

"Ohhhhh!" The brightness, a conflagration parenthesized by blackness, burned its vivid impression on her retina and sizzled into her brain.

"Melissa?"

"The light!" she protested.

"A fire," he explained and thanked God she, no matter her

state, had at least regained consciousness. His inability to rouse
her had worried him. The two bumps on her head, one on her
right temple and one at the back, neither of which broke the
skin, had been his main concern. She probably had a
concussion, maybe worse; if that were the case, Christian was
ill-equipped to help, when to help was his greatest impulse at the
moment. There was something tenderly vulnerable about this
woman, cupped as she was in his arms to share his warmth and
the warmth from the fire. It was a vulnerability he hadn't
noticed in the presence of Elizabeth, nor in the helicopter before
and after the crash, and it triggered protective instincts inside
him.

"Fire?" she asked. Yes, it did feel like a fire. It even sounded
like a fire. But its brightness was what continued to disturb her,
and its size. Was he burning a whole forest to warm her?

She located the knots raised on her skull. Her head hurt and
her vision was distorted.

"Any bump on the head is something to be taken seriously.
The sooner we get you out of here and to a doctor, the better."

"How exactly did we get here?" She still wanted to know
about the fire, but this seemed suddenly more important.

"You, I, and the wreckage, went over a fairly sizable
waterfall. You and I washed up not far from here; the
helicopter and meteorite weren't so lucky. I know it might seem
a strange thing to call us lucky, considering what we've been
through but it could be much worse."

"Except, there's still plenty of time for the worst to occur."
She didn't want to be a pessimist, but it seemed important she
distinguish reality from pipe dreams. "We can't stay here."

"You see that, too, do you? Another good sign!"

"It's unlikely anyone is going to spot us down here at the
bottom of this ravine." Faulty vision or not, she *could* see that
much. "Especially not if the weather stays rotten. So, this does
seem to be the exception to the general rule that surviors should

stay at the scene of the crash."

"I agree."

"The waterfall is an additional incentive to leave." She could feel its spray even if Christian had moved them into a spot sheltered from it. "Early settlers, as well as indigenous Indian populations, used to camp by waterfalls so the enemy couldn't distinguish smoke from the spray. I forget where I read that." She wondered if forgetting the source was more important than she'd like to think.

"So much for the advantages, beyond heat, of this particular camp fire."

"So, it's up the cliff. Find a clearing, flag down one of the rescue choppers, and, from there, it's only a few minutes air time to a Vancouver hospital."

"Wrong only in that it'll be air time to Feaswell Clinic."

"*The* Feaswell Clinic?" Melissa estimated the combined balance of her savings and checking accounts; she didn't think the total nearly sufficient to entice Feaswell, doctor or clinic, to take her on as either an in- or out-patient. When the Sultan of oil-rich Fhalan, in Vancouver for the World's Fair, had come down with appendecitis, he'd been rushed to the Feaswell. At the time, a popular "aside" had been the hopes that the mere billionaire had enough cash reserves to cover his bill.

"John Feaswell's a frat brother from Princeton."

"No reflection on your school, but I think Vancouver General will fit my pocketbook far better all the same."

"It'll be on the house. John owes me."

"I can pay for my own treatment," she insisted. Then, she modified: "Provided it's at Vancouver General."

"We'll see." With all her banter Melissa might have sounded as if she were back to normal, but he could tell, by the recurring pain lines across her forehead, that wasn't the case. There was something about her eyes, too, that worried him: a certain unfocused quality that shouldn't have been there.

"About this wonderful fire," she said, having come full circle. It was important she continue to be lucid. "Lightning took pity on two lost souls, did it?"

"Fire comes to you courtesy of one of dad's hand-crafted survival knives." He tapped the blade secured in its scabbard at his waist. "The hollow handle contains a compass, wire saw blade, waterproof matches: everything needed in a pinch, by any man or woman stranded in the middle of nowhere. I bought it back just last month from its original owner, a hunter in Idaho who swore by it for ten years."

"I take back any derogatory things I ever said about knives."

"You said a few derogatory things?" Christian was curious. 'My father and yours made such a good team producing collection-quality knives that I find it unusual you haven't been more eager to experiment along those same lines? If just from the financial potential. Then again, with your galleries in Canada and the U.S., you apparently haven't suffered from your reluctance to dabble in the weapons market. So, is it more a case of 'Why should I, when I don't have to?' "

"I see the more interesting question as, 'How did *you* get turned on to them?' " Turnabout was fair play.

"Which you and Elizabeth find strange because of my father's murder?"

Another stab of pain joined the battle waging inside Melissa's head, but she tried to ignore it in anticipation of the insights Christian might give her that he'd denied Elizabeth.

"Wasn't he murdered by one of his own knives?" Her trauma made her more brazen than she would have thought possible. Now, twisted reasoning or not, she felt what they'd been through gave her certain rights.

"People whose relatives die in plane crashes don't necessarily stop flying." The rest of his answer had to be just as carefully thought out. He found this woman attractive, and whatever that potential, he didn't want to spoil it by giving her the

impression he was in anyway mentally unbalanced, especially in
a life-and-death situation like this one. It was important they
totally trust and rely upon one another. On the other hand,
there were things he didn't dare reveal for fear they would even
superficially involve her in something she would undoubtedly
view as far too dangerous for whatever she could possibly hope
to get out of it. "Did you quit skiing when your mother had her
skiing accident?"

His reference to that personal tragedy made Melissa's head
hurt even more. "You know about my mother?"

"I subscribe to *Blade.*"

Blade was the must-read magazine for anyone even vaguely
interested in cutlery, as a business or for pleasure. Even Melissa
subscribed, not because she was "into" knives, but because there
were often related articles on subjects she found of interest,
from both a business and personal standpoint.

"There was a brief in-memoriam," Christian reminded her
" 'Wife of *Blade* hall-of-famer Charlie Jordan died this January
. . .' and all." Melissa had read and appreciated the black-
bordered notice printed by the magazine's editorial staff.

"Sorry to cramp your reasoning, but I did quit skiing after
my mother died." She didn't add how she'd never been any good
on skiis, always surprised whenever she reached the bottom of a
slope alive. How ironic it had been her mother, who'd so
relished the sport, who'd been killed by it.

He pulled her closer, not least of all because he liked the feel
of her in his arms. However, it was, also, a delaying tactic. It
was probably better to put this conversation to rest until he was
less rattled himself. He wouldn't admit it to Melissa, she had
enough to worry about, but he had trouble keeping his own
thoughts focused.

"Mmmmmm," she moaned softly; suddenly, exhaustion,
always in the race, gave every indication of overtaking her.

At first, Christian thought she'd fainted, but he was

reassured by her even breathing and the good color the warmth had returned to her cheeks. "You sleep," he told her, grateful she wasn't going to press him for answers.

She groaned softly, once again, and he was disturbed by the pain lines that remained on her face even as she dozed. He tried unsuccessfully to smooth them away with the tips of his fingers, but they defied all his efforts to erase them. Even with them, she was beautiful, and he wondered if he, like Prince Charming, could revive her with a kiss. The real question: revive her to what? She was far better momentarily removed from the reality, no matter how restless her sleep was.

And what about *his* reality, thoughts of which gave him a chill? In a way, he could envy this woman, because, once this episode ended favorably, she would return to her normal life, doing normal things. His personal horror, however, would extend far beyond the boundaries of this damp, mist-filled ravine. What he faced within the world outside was so malevolent it might well make this brief interlude seem mere child's play.

She was in trouble long before they topped the pathway that led out of the gorge and into the high-standing timber up top. It began with the loss of her peripheral vision. Then, what little vision she had left began to fade, and if all of that wasn't enough, the ever-present pain behind her eyes burrowed even deeper.

She would have voiced her growing concern but for her conscious effort to keep quiet at least until they were off the cliff face. Even though they'd spotted bears, had Christian known of her worsening condition, he would have stopped. The chances of running into a bear headed down the narrow trail for a meal on riverside berries became stacked more in the bear's favor with each even short delay.

"We'll take a long break as soon as we top out," he assured her, during one of those times neither of them could have taken another step without a breather. He could tell just by looking at her that she was in bad shape; but he, also, knew that whatever her condition, she would be better off if she could just make it up the steep incline. Once at the top, if worse came to worst, he'd carry her the rest of the way. Carrying her here, though, would require a slow and labored pace that with the attending threat of bears was best avoided.

Melissa never knew what inner sense of survival allowed her to make the final effort required to follow him under her own steam, up and out of that hole. Shortly after Christian assured that a long break awaited them at the summit, there commenced a chunk of Melissa's life that would, forever after, be recalled piecemeal. A loss of all vision; more and greater pain; a piggy-back ride, her ankles tied around Christian's waist with strips torn from his T-shirt, her hands tied around his neck; his assurances that there was a clearing not far ahead; a camp fire; another camp fire; and at that moment of ultimate hope, when he proclaimed a helicopter somewhere in the breaking cloud cover, something undefined tore loose inside of her and cast her adrift in a void without sight or sound.

2

"Virtual days of my life a blur and a blank!" Melissa complained to Carol Westingham who sat on the chair beside the bed. "What's more, after five complete days of unconsciousness, I can't believe I continue to drop off to sleep at the drop of a hat. Dr. Feaswell, of course, has his explanations; 'There is sleep, and then, there is sleep.' Christian, on the other hand, quite awake, was discharged two days ago."

"Isn't five days a long time to be comatose?" Carol asked. Her obvious concern, at the moment, though, was Kevin Silner who sat stiffly in the chair beside her.

Melissa shared Carol's concern. Kevin looked far more haggard than she did. After finally having access to a mirror, Melissa had decided she didn't look that bad—everything considered. Frankly, she'd been surprised to see Kevin at all, let alone in a hospital. As long as she'd known him, he'd exhibited definite anti-social behavior. After his having spent so much post Vietnam War time in medical facilities, he didn't put *any* hospital at the top of his must-visit list.

"Kevin, I really will understand if you want to cut your visit short." Her willingness to give him early leave took precedent over giving Carol a detailed rundown of her medical history. She'd see a lot more of her over the next few days in order to get brought up on business, Carol had carried most of the managerial work load since Melissa began tackling meteorites, crash landings, waterfalls, and all similar ilk.

"I'm fine," Kevin assured her and tried to run his fingers through his matted red hair.

Melissa didn't believe him, determined to give him another chance to exit before too many more minutes passed. She turned back to Carol but kept Kevin focused in her peripheral vision which, thank God, had returned as good as new. "The good Dr. Feaswell says that there are times when the body is subjected to so much stress in so short a time, that the brain overloads much as a computer does. In such cases, there's an equivalent shutdown of all systems. The length of time the computer/brain is down depends upon how long it takes for circuitry to get back to normal. In the case of an IBM terminal, a repair team comes in. In the case of the human brain, it has this miraculous ability to self-repair. Sometimes that self-repair takes a few hours; sometimes a few days; less often, years."

"You look in surprisingly great shape for someone who has been through what you've been through." Carol nodded toward the file folder of news clippings she'd brought for Melissa to see. "The papers were filled with the story. Which you might be happy to hear has been great for the gallery business."

"It's hard to find consolation in anything when you're hiding as many black-and-blue marks as I am. Although, a nurse assures me they've faded considerably from what they were just days ago."

"Well, take as long as you need for a complete recovery," Carol insisted. "I'll continue holding the fort."

"I really don't know what I'd do without you, you know that, don't you?" It was hard to believe it was only two years ago that Carol had dropped by the Gastown gallery with some dried-weed arrangements which really hadn't been up to the standards of the rest of Melissa's inventory. She'd accepted that obvious fact with remarkably good grace, back the next day with some work by a friend too shy to come in himself which she thought Melissa might find of more interest. She'd been right. Melissa had bought all three pieces of the bone filigree by Kevin Silner. Up until a year after Melissa had started to sell his work on a regular basis, and for at least six months after Melissa had hired Carol full-time, Kevin had remained an unseen entity.

"Flattery will get you anything," Carol said.

Melissa brought Kevin into the conversation, rather than let him sit there and stew on where he was. "Carol's kept you busy, has she?"

"I brought you a get-well gift," he said and fished the front pocket of his faded, Swiss-cheese ragged jeans. He had fine-boned, long, delicate, but highly callused artist's hands. He retrieved the wad of crumpled blue cloth and proceeded to unfold it carefully on his lap.

"Oh, Kevin, it's beautiful!" The necklace was a circle of two-inch wide, one-inch long, interlocked, curved panels of filigreed bone that portrayed one run-on Oriental river scene: palms, sampans, figures with open umbrellas . . . Had she not known, she never would have guessed that what she had in her hand was made from something as insignificant as artifically bleached breastbone of turkey.

"You really like it?" he asked and handed it over for closer inspection.

"It has to be your best piece yet," she said and not to inflate his ego; although, she did enjoy the way his usual somberness dissolved when his work was involved. His oak-brown eyes literally took on a new life that made Melissa wonder, not for the first time, about the young man from whom this world-weary "old" man had evolved.

"He insisted he bring it personally," Carol said and sounded as if she still didn't quite believe he'd carried through.

"Which makes it all the more special," Melissa said, even more impressed by the work in close-up. She turned its lace-like lightness in her fingers and tried to calculate the man-hours spent in patiently working each and every hole into the bone so the total picture emerged so perfectly in between. It seemed impossible that a material so common could have been converted, even by craftsmanship, into something so wonderfully gossamer. She'd tried to persuade Kevin to try his hand at working ivory, even offering to absorb the expense of some practice material so he wouldn't have to worry about the cost of early mistakes, but he'd declined. What's more, Melissa had since decided he was right: why mess with a good thing?

"I suppose we should really head out," Carol said, "Karen Timms is bringing in some carvings this afternoon. She asked about you, by the way. Most of your artists and regulars have. They're waiting to hear if you're up to visitors."

"Actually, I have hopes of being up and out of here even faster than Dr. Feaswell expects," Melissa said.

"Well, don't do anything foolish," Carol warned. "Somehow, we'll continue to plod along without you."

As much as Melissa might like to think her business would grind to a halt without her speedy return, she knew Carol probably did have things well under control. Her real anxiousness to leave had more to do with her own aversion to hospitals. She'd spent many agonizing hours in one, while her father lay dying. The Feaswell Clinic might have better pictures on its walls than Vancouver General, and its staff might run around in designer smocks and uniforms, but it was still a hospital.

"Thank you both for coming," she said, extending a hand to

Kevin who, with seeming reluctance, took it. "And, thank you
again for this truly exquisite gift. I'll cherish it always." She'd
been on the verge of magnanimously suggesting that he let her
exchange it for one of the smaller items he had on sale at her
downtown gallery. She was sure she could clear him a sizable
and immediate profit on this piece; however, his motivations
for creativity had never seemed to be financial.

Before Melissa, he had actually given away most of his
work, or traded it for the bare necessities. Even now, when she
knew he could budget to afford better, he continued to live in a
small apartment in a low-rent section of Chinatown inhabited
mainly by boat people the Canadian government had allowed
into the country during one of the mad exoduses out of
Southeast Asia. He spent his money on cigarettes and turkeys,
the latter which he ate and boiled down for their breastbones.
The rest, as far as Melissa could tell, went as handouts to other
U.S. veterans and defectors who had found their way to
Canada, both before and after the Vietnam War. Melissa had
been surprised to hear that a man who had lost so much of his
youth in the war had no qualms about giving his money to men
who had fled rather than join him in fighting it.

"Melissa?" He broke her rambling train of thought, and she
realized she still held his hand. She figured he was embarrassed
and wanted her to turn loose. When she released Kevin's
fingers; however, he held on.

"Kevin?" For some inexplicable reason, she experienced a
shiver, not unlike the many she'd experienced in the very recent
past.

"Get well." With a nervous glance in Carol's direction, he
turned loose of Melissa's hand.

She was confused. There had been something about the look
he'd given Carol that said what? Melissa always suspected the
two had a relationship that went deeper than friendship. Had he
thought Carol had somehow misconstrued the way Melissa had

held overly long to his fingers? Surely not! Carol knew both of them too well for such silliness.

"I'll drop by tomorrow," Carol promised. If she were in anyway disturbed, she didn't show it.

"I do love this!" Melissa said and brought the necklace to her cheek in final farewell to Kevin who followed Carol to the door. Did he linger far longer than Melissa would have expected? No, she was imagining things. Obviously, she needed a bit more time to pull herself completely together.

That thought in mind, she was genuinely surprised when, a few seconds later, the door opened and Kevin returned— without Carol.

"I told Carol I left my cigarettes," he said, although he hadn't once lit up while in the room. "I really wanted to tell you about Captain 'E.T.' "

"E.T.?" Melissa didn't have the vaguest idea where this was leading, unless he'd picked up a video of the Steven Spielberg sci-fi classic. Somehow, she couldn't imagine Kevin remaining to talk movies.

"I saw him," he said and came over to the bed. His brown eyes had a slightly fuzzy quality that Melissa suspected would remind Christian of her eyes on that ride down the river in the wrecked helicopter. Was Kevin on drugs? Had that always, no matter what Carol insisted, continued to be part of his problem? "I saw him," he repeated. He looked as if were genuinely expecting her to give some kind of startled reaction. "What's more, *he* saw *me!*"

"Kevin, I really . . ." She wanted to apologize but didn't know for what.

The door opened. Melissa hoped it was Carol. It wasn't.

"So, it's about time you rejoined the living!" Elizabeth exclaimed in a loud greeting.

Kevin did an about-face, and he hurried from the room. In leaving, he almost knocked down the U.S. army colonel whom

Elizabeth had brought with her.

"A man in a hurry, if ever I saw one!" Elizabeth judged. She came to the bed, followed by the colonel who looked unfazed by Kevin and their near collision.

"He's not overly fond of hospitals," Melissa excused him. Something continued to tell her it had to do with more than just hospitals. What, though, did it have to do with E.T. and her?

"If he reacts that way to them now, what'll be his reaction when he reaches my ripe old age?" Elizabeth looked no less rumpled than when in the woods. She'd buttoned her blouse all wrong; the errant button-without-an-apparent-hole glared from her collar. Her skirt was askew. Her gray hair, drier than when Melissa last saw it, sprouted three geyser-like tufts.

By comparison, the colonel was immaculate: not a hair, nor a piece of his uniform out of place. His shoes were so spit-shined, Melissa suspected she could see her reflection in them. His almost fatherly, trust-me look was emphasized by his short, salt-and-pepper hair, and his big, basset-hound brown eyes. Although obviously shaved, and probably recently, his cheeks and chin already had a natural shadow that gave the impression he'd stayed up late into the night to shoulder the latest burdens of the world.

"Colonel Sampson," Elizabeth said.

"We crashed in your helicopter?" Melissa asked.

He smiled a smile neither too restrained, nor too broad: a friendly but seemingly well-rehearsed smile. "Actually, the helicopter was *officially* the property of the U.S. taxpayer." His voice was baritone, full and melodious. It carried well; if louder, it might easily slide through whatever the noises of a battlefield. "I merely arranged for its use. Liaison, we call it."

"Elizabeth's use? CanTech's use?"

"I've come to think of Elizabeth *as* CanTech."

"Stuff and nonsense!" Elizabeth responded to the flattery.

Melissa's impression was that this Sampson had this "Delilah" well in hand.

"I'm afraid there's really very little I can tell you, or the American taxpayer, about the loss of your helicopter, Colonel Sampson. It crashed, got washed down a river and over a falls. One minute, it was in the sky; the next minute . . ." Melissa shrugged.

"Maybe the colonel can tell *you* a bit," Elizabeth said cryptically. Then, she explained, "He's sent in a team of experts to look over the crash site." She waved a hand in front of her face, as if to harass some unseen irritant. "The team would have been on-site sooner, of course, if it had had the cooperation of your friend, Christian Wynard."

Melissa didn't like the sound of *your friend*. "I'm afraid I don't follow."

"Immediately upon return, Christian was put under Dr. Feaswell's personal care," Elizabeth said. "Feaswell insisted he was medically unfit to see anyone for three days."

"With him unavailable, and you comatose, we had no success locating your crash site," Colonel Sampson explained. "You had covered a surprisingly good distance on foot; the wreckage was scattered and not readily observable from the air; and the weather stayed frustratingly erratic after you were airlifted to safety. It was only after Dr. Feaswell allowed us access to Mr. Wynard that we actually pinpointed the area."

"There's a problem with that?" Melissa knew one was insinuated.

"Well," Elizabeth said noncommittally. She seemed momentarily distracted by the file folder her fingers had found while "walking" the Kleenex box, and other hospital paraphernalia on the bedside stand.

"A business associate thought I might be interested in reading the details," Melissa identified the clippings. "So far, I've remained content with just having lived them."

"I don't suppose there's anything in here about the press

conference Christian called this morning." Elizabeth thumbed
through the top clippings; Melissa caught sight of a picture of
the rescue helicopter, its stretcher being unloaded. Elizabeth
closed the folder and tapped it with fingers gnarled by years of
digging "treasure" from the ground. "No. His conference won't
make the papers until this evening; although, I believe it made
all the networks' morning news."

Melissa had been too caught up in her return to life to watch
T.V., and she said so.

"Seems he's gotten himself a meteorite," Elizabeth said, "A
Mr. Candive in Nova Scotia just happened to pick one up when
it dropped from the sky in nineteen-twenty-two. Held onto it
for all these years. A stony-iron meteorite just waiting for
Christian Wynard to come along with his fat pocketbook." She
locked eyes with Melissa. "Christian, you, the colonel, and I
know what's made from iron, don't we?"

"Steel," Melissa obliged.

"A knife blade," Elizabeth was more specific. "Which is
exactly what Christian told the press he plans to make of it."

"You're surprised?" How could she be? At the recovery site,
Elizabeth had as much as accused Christian of wanting that
meteorite to use for a custom-made knife blade.

"Not surprised by *what* he plans to do with it," Elizabeth
confirmed. "Surprised by the appearance of this particular
meteorite, at this particular time."

Elizabeth's pause invited comment. even the colonel looked
expectant. Melissa was reminded of Kevin who had, likewise,
waited. She'd had no satisfactory response for him, either.

"Well." She took a deep breath and decided to make a try.
"My father picked up two meteorites in nineteen-fifty-four."
Which Melissa suspected they both knew, too; which meant,
this wasn't the conclusion either of them wanted. "He held onto
both until Christian's father showed up over twenty-five years
later." She didn't mention Kyle Wynard's fat pocketbook,

because that relationship had been based on mutual friendship and a mutual love of knives, *not* cash and carry.

"Likewise, Mr. Candive chooses this particular moment to step forward, meteorite in outstretched hands?" There was no mistaking Elizabeth's skepticism. Insinuating what?

"The publicity probably told Mr. Candive what a jackpot he had in his backyard." Melissa didn't need a score card to tell Elizabeth gave her all failing marks for that attempt.

"I told the colonel your attraction to Christian was likely to taint your judgment of him," Elizabeth said.

Attracted to him or not, Melissa hated to let the accusation stand. "It might help if you both were less obtuse."

"There, there." The colonel's voice was calm and soothing. Without saying as much, in so many words, it requested both women to be very careful they didn't say something for which they'd be sorry later.

"I just met the man!" Melissa insisted. If she were uneasy, it was because she had a hard time separating what she now felt for Christian from what she'd felt at the time. There was no way two people could go through what they had gone through without drawing somewhat closer together. "Our fathers worked on various projects, but, at the time, I was away at college, and Christian, I believe, was in Japan getting down the basics of aquaculture."

"I think we drift a bit from the point," the colonel said, trying to pacify her.

But Melissa would have none of it. "What exactly *is* the point?" she demanded.

Apparently used to formidable opponents, he took her request not as the sarcasm it was intended to be, but as a reasonable request that deserved an answer. "We're concerned Mr. Wynard has bilked us out of our rightful property."

" 'Our,' meaning CanTech and the U.S. government?" Melissa wanted to know. She didn't see what this had to do with her. " 'Our,' meaning your and Elizabeth's property?"

"Look here, Melissa . . ." Elizabeth was silenced by the hand, no matter how lightly, that the colonel placed on her arm.

"It boils down to what's fair," Colonel Sampson filled the abrupt silence. "What you view as fair, Melissa. What I view as fair. What Elizabeth, CanTech, the Canadian and the U.S. governments view as fair. And, in the end, what Christian Wynard views as fair."

"I hardly see what's unfair about some man who comes out of the blue to sell Christian a rock that's been sitting in some backyard for sixty-some years."

"Nor do Elizabeth and I," he said. "Do we Elizabeth?"

"No," she begrudgingly admitted: a second surprise.

Melissa asked herself if she'd buy a used car from either of these people, and decided she'd have to think long and hard about it. Strange how her opinion of Elizabeth had changed in so short a time.

"What we *do* find unfair," the colonel continued, "is even the possibility that Mr. Candive hasn't really sat on his meteorite all of these years but only recently happened upon it."

"Like within the last few days!" Elizabeth oozed venom.

"Why don't you two quit beating around the bush!" Melissa wasn't up to whatever guessing games they were putting her through.

"It's *my* meteorite! And I need it for research." Elizabeth exploded, another tuft of her hair puffed from her head like Old Faithful in full eruption. Her glasses slid the full length of her nose and would have slipped off if she hadn't stopped them. *"Christian* stole it!" There was no tolerance for the competition. "And he only wants it for knife-blades."

"You had to know this day would come," Melissa reminded them. She suspected she still was missing something and she wished she had a moment or two to herself to figure it out.

"Not *this* day!" Elizabeth begged to differ. She looked as if her patience had run out.

Once again, it was calm, cool, Colonel Sampson to the rescue. "We expected he might *one* day beat us to a meteorite touchdown, or *one* day offer financial enticement to persuade some scientist or layman to sell him what they'd beat us to."

"Isn't that what happened?" She was lost again.

"That's *the story!*" Elizabeth pressed home. She seemed barely under control.

"We've been unable to locate our meteorite at the crash site." The colonel sounded as if anyone with a modicum of intelligence could now put two and two together after being given so much of the equation.

Melissa, brain-rattled or not, hadn't lost all reason. "Talk about a needle in a haystack, let's talk about the rocks in that ravine, all the pieces that meteorite could have broken into, all the miles any of those pieces could have been washed by that powerhouse river. Is it any wonder you can't find it?"

"Someone was there after you left but before the colonel's investigatory team got there," Elizabeth said. "That means, someone was there during the three days Christian was under the doctor's care." Each word, slow and concise, hammered home the implications. "Coincidence?"

"How do you know someone was there?" Christian wasn't there to defend himself, and Melissa wasn't about to take anything said against him at merely face value.

"There are ways to tell such things," Colonel Sampson said all-knowingly, the wizened guru who expected disciples everywhere to accept his word as gospel.

"How *do you know?*" she insisted.

"A breath-mint wrapper, for one."

"Did you ask if I had any breath mints out there?"

"No need to ask, unless you washed up on one side of the falls, ate your breath mint, discarded its wrapper, reentered the water, and swam to the opposite shore. A Herculean feat, Miss

Jordan!" With all the potential for sarcasm, he somehow came across sincere. A knack Melissa thought qualified him for diplomatic service.

"Poachers? Campers? Hikers?" Melissa suggested.

"Maybe." The slight tilt of his head emphasized an openness for any suggestions but insinuated her suggestions weren't really as good as his, especially when calculating the odds of any poacher, camper, or hiker appearing in that particular hole, during any one or more of the particular three days in question. "I suppose that might even account for all the recent footprints, other than Christian and yours, that we came up with."

"My foot!" Elizabeth exclaimed; Melissa wondered if this was some kind of bad-cop, good-cop routine: one screamed and shouted to make the suspect nervous, the other good-manneredly put the suspect off guard; except, Melissa had nothing to tell them. She'd come out of that pit comatose and had stayed that way, on and off, for days.

"We're not *officially* accusing Mr. Wynard, you understand." Melissa's look of incredulity made even the colonel come up with an atypical yes-I-know-*that*-does-sound-contradictory grin.

"What do you mean, we're not . . .?" Elizabeth was still enough under his sway to be brought up short under the impact of his get-a-grip-on-yourself glare.

"While we don't mind losing fairly, we don't take kindly to cheats," the colonel proceeded calmly. "What we hope to ascertain is whether or not Mr. Wynard is, indeed, a cheat."

"I really *can* be a good loser, Melissa," Elizabeth insisted. "I just want to make sure I lose fairly."

"I'm not going to ask what any of this has to do with me, because I'm not at all sure I want to know."

"I don't believe that!" The colonel looked just like Melissa's father had always looked whenever Melissa had set a course divergent from his own.

"It's between you, Christian, CanTech, the Canadian and U.S. governments."

"What about all your personal efforts on Elizabeth's behalf?" he asked. "Don't you feel cheated in having won the game with maybe someone else getting the prize?"

"All we want you to do is persuade him to let you take a look." Suddenly, Elizabeth was peaches and cream. She smoothed her hair in a seeming attempt to make herself appear less volatile.

"Why don't one of you just ask to see it?"

"We have!" Elizabeth's just-smoothed hair puffed like a dandelion gone to seed.

"He's not cooperative." The colonel sounded as if the only explanation for *that* had to be nefarious.

"Isn't he required to cooperate?"

"Required?" The colonel looked genuinely nonplussed. "How? By whom?"

"By you," Melissa spelled it out. His who-me act was his least convincing. "By the U.S. government."

"We have no authority to require any Canadian citizen to do anything. Had we, I'd be demanding your cooperation, not asking for it."

"What about demands by CanTech or the Canadian government?"

"Mr. Wynard is very wealthy, very influential, very well-respected . . ." He stopped, seemed to reconsider, started again: "No one wants to call undue attention to U.S.-Canadian-CanTech involvement in any of this. Some people feel what publicity we've already had is detrimental to the low profile most of us involved in this would prefer to keep."

"What is there about you and CanTech that can't take a little public scrutiny?" Where it hadn't mattered so much before, Melissa saw it mattering more and more.

"Classified!" Elizabeth answered: a Pavlov dog conditioned

to automatic response.

Colonel Sampson, however, apparently recognized Melissa as not likely satisfied by that answer, nor by any vague references to national security. "CanTech performs a whole range of research. As there are so few networks, world-wide, set up to explore the sky's seemingly aberrant phenomena, the U.S. government naturally maintains close ties, whenever possible, with those who do. I'm sure you recognize, Melissa, the scientific and military advantages of isolating any exotic, non-earth-originating metals that have the capacity to withstand the high temperatures of any entry through our atmosphere."

"That's what you're after?"

"I'm merely pointing out some possibilities. CanTech is better known for its involvement in cataloguing and investigating U.F.O. sightings in upper North America, which the U.S. finds of interest from a security-of-our-northern-frontier standpoint."

"Flying saucers and little green men, you mean?"

"Flying saucers and little green men, I *don't* mean!" the colonel emphasized; Elizabeth looked as if Melissa were someone who regularly shopped *MOTHER HAS MARTIAN BABY* tabloids at the local supermarket. "Despite all consistent rumors, I can truthfully say, neither CanTech, nor any other similar research facility I know of, has ever found concrete proof of life, intelligent or otherwise, elsewhere in the known universe."

"No mysterious, alien aircraft and pilots in Lab Ten?" She couldn't really remember if it were Lab Ten, Eight, Seven, or what, the news had once reported.

"Remember that story, do you?" Then, as if she might not remember enough, he continued, "Alien spacecraft down in the Klondike. Aliens aboard, airlifted to CanTech facilities for physiological studies. All lies. All ridiculous. But, a prime example of why a lot of people prefer to keep the press at arm's-length. The notoriety of that one, patently absurd story had newsmen literally camping outside the CanTech gates and following the scientists home at night. More than a few of those same scientists, who found that attention so disruptive, see this misunderstanding with Mr. Wynard as having all potential for similar disruption to their lives and work schedules."

"Others of us aren't so thin-skinned!" Elizabeth injected; the colonel's frown didn't encourage her to elaborate.

"All we want is for you to look at this Nova Scotia meteorite." He made it sound the most reasonable request in the world. "You saw *our* meteorite at the camp site."

"After all *your* meteorite went through, what makes you think it'll look anything like when I last saw it, even if it is one and the same?"

"If you can't make a positive identification, you tell us. That's all."

"And if I can?"

"Either way, a decision will be made. Possibly, Mr. Wynard will simply be allowed to keep his ill-begotten gain, rather than risk further fuss."

"Never!" Elizabeth contradicted. If looks could kill, the colonel's would have killed her for the outburst.

"I can't believe Christian's involved in any attempt to bilk you, or anyone else, out of a hunk of stone!" Nevertheless, she remembered the high price he'd supposedly paid Brandywine Timber for right of recovery had the meteorite gone down on Brandywine land. "You can learn a lot about a man when you've been through what I've been through with this one."

"Then, you should be pleased at a chance to prove your character judgment correct."

Melissa knew she'd walked head-on into that one.

"And if he doesn't choose to show me this Nova Scotia meteorite? He does, after all, know I'll recognize it as a fraud if it's recognizable at all."

"If he won't show you, and he won't show us, we'll have to surmise the why, won't we? It's called deductive reasoning, based on circumstantial evidence, and it's done every day."

The phone rang. Melissa reached for it and hoped it was Christian whom she could count upon to get her out of this, like he'd gotten her out of that other confusing spot. It wasn't.

"For you, Colonel," she said and handed it over.

"Colonel Sampson," he spoke into the mouthpiece. If he said nothing more until his concluding, "thank-you," the change of his expression from placid to flushed said a good deal.

Melissa never dreamed she'd be made privy to the disturbing substance of his conversation. She was, therefore, surprised when, without preamble, he said, quite angrily: "It would seem our helicopter, Miss Jordan, came down not by any act of God, but because someone, very human, took precise pains to see it died in the sky."

"Yes, *of course,* sabotage!" For Elizabeth, all the pieces were apparently in place, the promised picture revealed.

"You're *not* insinuating Christian, to get his hands on your meteorite, somehow planted a bomb on board?" Melissa made it sound as incredulous as she found it. "Then, he blasély steps inside for a ride?"

"Shrapnel pattern and powder burns on the pilot's body . . ."

"The pilot!" Melissa's interruption was automatic, triggered partly by guilt. Except for that brief moment on board the wreckage, washed downriver, she'd pretty much put the pilot completely out of her mind.

"Captain Steven Miller." Elizabeth's inference was that Melissa might well have shown more concern for him, less for Christian Wynàrd.

"We have the pilot's body." The colonel's voice was back to neutral. "Killed, though, not by impact but by some kind of explosion before any of you reached the ground. The bomb—

or, bombs, since there's evidence that there may have been more than one—could have been small and affixed specifically to take out the pilot and/or all engine capabilities."

"Sparing the meteorite and specific passenger!" Elizabeth pointed out. "Sparing *you* by accident."

"You can't drum up a meteorite, but you can come up with conclusive evidence of an exploded bomb, or bombs?"

"Men whose profession is war are well-trained to detect even the most miniscule evidence of their trade."

"It was pure luck we survived the drop," Melissa said. "I find it hard to believe Christian would risk his life, my life, and kill a man, for a piece of stone, by coming down blind anywhere in that rugged terrain in that kind of weather."

"He lived!" Elizabeth obviously wasn't won over. "You lived! The pilot didn't die from the fall. I say, the meteorite survived, and Christian now has it."

"All for a hunk of stone?" Melissa remained disbelieving.

"The man has a demon loose inside him!" said Elizabeth-turned-psychiatrist.

"Did I mention how the chopper came down on Brandywine Timber land?" he said, thereby dropping a sort of bomb of his own. "Granted, that could be another coincidence."

"Humph!" Elizabeth expelled air in readable disbelief.

"It having done so," the colonel continued, "certainly held out the opportunity for the introduction of some interesting legal implications."

"Did it?" Melissa asked.

"There's some thought he might even have evoked 'Rights of Salvage,' if it were argued the wreckage and cargo, once down, were abandoned. Of course, I'm not a legal-eagle and can't tell you if any such arguments would stand up in court. Moot points, anyway, since Christian hasn't publicly laid claim to *that* meteorite but to one from Nova Scotia."

"Look," Melissa argued, "just when was he supposed to

plant these bombs? Not when he got on, because he was with me every second. To have hired someone to do it earlier doesn't seem practical unless he could, somehow, have known beforehand that there wasn't going to be more possible survivors to keep him from walking off with the prize. For all he knew, all of us could have been leaving on that helicopter."

"Anyone who killed the pilot could as easily killed however many survivors."

Melissa was appalled by Elizabeth's suggestion. "He didn't kill me, *did he!*"

"With you, he could afford to play hero." Elizabeth wasn't giving an inch. "In your condition, you weren't going to give directions to the crash site. He correctly figured he had plenty of time to send in an extraction crew."

"His motivations, for all this: iron for steel; steel for knife? Unbelievable!"

"Truth is often stranger than fiction, my dear." Elizabeth's attitude was definitely as-a-scientist-I-should-know. "His father was brutally murdered, and Christian discovered his father's body. Knowing all of that, can you see this compulsion of a successful aquaculturist *and* successful sculptor to follow in his father's knife-making footsteps as anything *but* abnormal?"

"If your father died in a plane accident, would you never fly?" Melissa found it ironic she was using the same argument Christian had used with her.

"I think that just might be the case!" It wasn't the answer Melissa wanted to hear. Nor was Elizabeth's follow-up. "A possibly better question: would you never ski again if your mother died in a skiing accident?"

Melissa experienced an unnerving chill of dèjá vu.

"There are arguments to be made on both sides," the colonel said. "There are *always* arguments to support both sides. And, I do hope to make it perfectly clear . . ." He flashed Elizabeth a look that warned her not to inject something here. ". . . that we might do Christian a grave injustice by harboring our suspicions. On the other hand, such suspicions do exist, and we do him and ourselves an even greater disservice by not setting them right. His indifference shouldn't deter our every effort to clear our own collective conscience."

"I agree!" Elizabeth said, although everyone knew he would have preferred the same response from Melissa.

"Why don't you sleep on what I've said, Melissa?" the colonel suggested.

The colonel obviously suspected that had Melissa at that moment been forced into a definite commitment, she'd have been less than the cooperative agent he'd thought to enlist.

"After you've slept on it, give us your decision, and we'll abide by it, no questions asked. No matter how Christian sees it, our object isn't harassment, but to find answers to questions that are better off answered."

Elizabeth looked as if she were going to say something but thought better.

"Would it be all right to call you sometime tomorrow for your answer?" the colonel diplomatically asked.

"Yes, that'll be fine." She would have preferred the whole thing to go away, but she was pragmatist enough to know it wasn't going anywhere.

The door opened to admit a clinic-smocked orderly.

"In the meantime, I suspect this gentleman is here to tell us we've overstayed our visiting privileges." The colonel prepared for diplomatic exit.

"Yes," the orderly agreed and opened his work garment to reveal the machine gun concealed underneath.

Within a mere fraction of a second, the gun was swung up, positioned, and spewing a staccato of bullets into the room.

Unadulterated instinct launched Melissa off the bed and put it between her and the gunman. It was inbred reflex, honed by her survival training in the woods. As the inner jolt propelled her off the bed, she screamed in automatic response—a sounding of frustration, of anger, or fear, a need to drown the horror with sounds of her own.

She plunged into a world of sensations: the rat-a-tat-tat noise, the splintering glass and wood, the splattering plaster, the thudding bullets swallowed by mattress and pillow, the zinging metal projectiles in deadly ricochet.

3

She thought she was either dead or dying. No matter her agility in leaving the bed and covers. She had calculated her odds, in one split second, and found them stacked against her.

When the noise stopped, the silence was an irritant.

She was dazed, crouched in a defensive ball around which stuffing from the bed, powdered-plaster rain, settled out of the air.

The window had exploded outward, but in so doing had left evidence behind; a move to her left or right and fragmented glass would have cut Melissa's knees.

"Don't bother with me!" someone ordered, "Ms. Howard is in bad shape, and Miss Jordan . . ."

"Melissa!"

She recognized both voices: the colonel and Christian. She doubted the reality of both. There was no way the colonel could have survived the barrage. As for Christian, he'd been discharged, off to make the mischief that had the colonel and

Elizabeth up in arms.

"Melissa!"

She didn't look up as Christian dropped beside her.

"Christian?" She didn't believe it, not even his arms folding her against him in reminiscence of their time spent fiercely fighting for survival in the wild. This wasn't wilderness. This was *the* Feaswell Clinic, *the* poshest address for the ailing rich in Vancouver, B.C. Shoot-outs simply didn't occur in such august surroundings.

"It's all right, Melissa! It's all right!"

Except, it wasn't all right. Someone had stepped nonchalantly into her hospital room, pulled out a machine gun and opened fire. Would she ever be the same?

"Elizabeth?" She didn't recognize her own voice.

"Not good, I'm afraid." He tried to help her to her feet, but she didn't budge. She wasn't ready for what lay beyond the bed.

"The colonel?"

"Some very nasty wounds."

"There were *thousands* of bullets. How could he have survived them?"

"His quick reflexes saved you both."

He wasn't just a pencil pusher, then. He had the responses of a bonafide warrior. He knew what the gun could do, and he knew how to launch a counteroffensive within the miniscule time allowed.

"Why?"

Christian misinterpreted her question. "The colonel had a gun and obviously knew how to use it."

Melissa hadn't noticed the colonel's gun. So much a part of his uniform? Someone so non-observant was lucky she'd recognized the enemy when she'd seen him.

"Why?" She couldn't expend energy for more words.

Christian was more attuned this time: "Why was the madman shooting? He won't be telling, because the colonel's one shot precludes any confessions. I suspect he was dead most of the time he was firing."

Melissa shuddered; her anger swelled. "What did I ever do to him?"

"Christian?" It was John Feaswell. "Here, let me get to her."

"No!" Melissa protested. Not yet. She wanted to be left alone, except for Christian. His arms were better than anything that even *the* John Feaswell, of *the* Feaswell Clinic, could prescribe.

"We have to make sure you're okay, Melissa," John insisted.

"I think she's fine, John, Just a little shaken."

"*Thinking* she's fine isn't enough. We've got to be sure. You've seen what we have in this room, and she could be wounded, bleeding internally and not even know it. Shock can mask the worst. So, kindly, let me to her. When I'm done, the two of you can cuddle to your hearts' content."

"He's right, Melissa," Christian agreed. "We have to be sure."

She took a big breath to summon resolve to compel an intelligent woman to act responsibly. In point of fact, if she *were* wounded, she didn't want to just sit there and die.

She let them help her to her feet. She didn't look at the activity in the other part of the room, she wasn't ready for the focal point.

"She's bleeding, John!"

"Just keep cool, Christian!" John insisted. "Or, I'll ask you to step out of the room until I'm finished."

"I'm bleeding." Melissa was fascinated by how the blood *was* blossomed near the hem of her hospital gown.

"It's superficial," John assured. "Now if you two will let me continue."

Christian leaned his mouth very close to her ear. "Be brave."

Melissa managed a smile. She was glad Christian was there. She needed his distraction.

"A couple of scratches," John finally diagnosed. "Amazing! Darned lucky, too, by the looks of this room. Speaking of which, I'd like Melissa moved to room 312." He looked at Christian whose worry lines were beginning to surface. "Think you can manage that, or shall I summon an orderly?"

"I've seen one too many of your orderlies." Melissa's attempt at levity coaxed a smile from Christian.

John was more serious. "You'll find he's not one of ours. I know all the Vietnam vets on my staff."

"Vietnam vet?" Melissa and Christian said in unison.

"I'll throw back the sheet if you'd like to see his *Nam Raider* tattoo."

"I'll pass," Melissa said.

"He came gunning for the colonel?" Christian asked.

"I'm just a medical doctor," John said. "You want motivation for murder, you need a psychiatrist's opinion, or a police investigator's. I suspect you'll have the latter very shortly."

A doctor beckoned from the doorway. John went over, and Melissa followed him with her eyes only as far as the sheet-draped body on the floor. She turned to Christian who gave her a reassuring hug. He put his mouth to her ear: "You'd never guess, but John has a very good bedside manner."

"This isn't a situation conducive to good anything," Melissa said.

John returned and asked, "Do either of you know the quickest way to reach Elizabeth Howard's next of kin?" He read their unasked question and answered it: "I'm surprised we salvaged two lives out of this."

"She has a sister in Lytton," Melissa replied. Two women didn't share five days together in a wilderness without learning something about one another. "Her husband and son died in a car accident over ten years ago."

"Thanks, I'll get someone on it," John said. "Then I'll send a nurse to room 312 with a sedative. Why don't the two of you see if you can beat her there? Out the door, to your right, approximately three doors . . ."

"Okay! I'm not *that* dense," Christian retorted.

"Just remember, Melissa out from sedation when the police arrive means she'll have a night's rest before the questions begin."

"*I* don't have any answers." Answers were what Melissa wanted as much as any policeman did.

"It's my experience," John said, "that a person without answers has never stopped the police, the world over, from asking the questions."

"Dr. Feaswell?" It was a nurse this time. "Mr. Twanli . . ."

"Seems the world goes on," John said wearily.

Melissa and Christian followed him around the sheet-covered body of the tattooed man and out into the hall.

Room 312 was decorated as tastefully as the room now in ruin had been. Melissa was sure every color, fabric, and stick of furniture had been chosen by experts to give the illusion that patients got their money's worth, at least as far as accommodations.

The nurse who joined them wasn't the one with the promised sedative. "The doctor recommends a shower; a tub bath may extend into police time."

"Yes, a shower." The doctor had to be psychic. Every bullet but one had missed her, and Melissa felt violated, more dirty than after days in the wilderness.

"This isn't exactly how I expected our reunion to go," Christian said.

Grasping his arm, Melissa said, "Did I thank you for hauling me out of the wilderness on your back?"

He gave her a tender smile. "Several times." He glanced at the nurse who made an impatient gesture. "We'll talk tomorrow."

"If I'm not here, which I don't plan to be, try my condo."

"John will want you here for at least a couple of days observation."

"He'll have to just want. I've had my fill of the Feaswell Clinic. I know killers aren't your frat brother's fault, but . . ."

To her surprise, Christian pulled her close aginst him and kissed her. She clung to him, returning his kiss. She wasn't ready to let him go. He offered her a stable sense of focus, in a world suddenly tilted. And the touch of his lips warmed her, sending shimmers of delight radiating through her body.

When he finally drew back, he said, "Now, I *really* don't want to go." He licked his lips as if to reclaim some lingering sensation of her kiss.

Reluctant or not, he left. Melissa took a quick shower in bathroom facilities that could compete with the best of hotel suites. A nurse gave her a tablet while a second nurse dressed the wound on her legs.

Her attention was caught by a man standing in the doorway. "A pretty small medal for what you went through." Inspector Roger Dwighton referred to her bandage. That, and his introduction, were the last things she remembered until morning.

"Nice rest?" The nurse pulled back the drapes to reveal another appropriately gloomy Vancouver day. Melissa's reply was noncommittal. Nothing about drug-induced sleep was as refreshing as the real thing.

The nurse presented a menu. As Melissa's experiences with the food had proved they were gourmet, she decided to stay for breakfast.

She ordered freshly squeezed orange juice and crepes. The ordinariness of such routine made it hard to imagine that only yesterday in a room down the hall, she'd faced a killer with a machine gun and survived the experience. She had to make it a point to thank . . . "Could you tell me Colonel Sampson's room?"

"He was transferred to the CanTech facilities last night."

"He's all right?"

"Stable."

Melissa breathed a sigh of relief. Although seeing him was no longer as easy as stopping on her way out, she put it at the top of her to-do list.

"I'll be checking out directly after breakfast."

The nurse looked doubtful. "Perhaps, I should have Dr. Feaswell stop by first?"

Melissa suspected John, after his part in the drama, was probably relaxing at home. She imagined wrong.

"Dr. Feaswell *is* in residence." He came through the doorway.

"On the scene, because Christian told me you might try to pull a disappearing act this morning." He came in the rest of the way. "Now, what's this about you not being sure Miss Westingham is capable of managing your business without you?"

"Carol, not capable? Nonsense!"

"Good! Because she looked eminently competent when I saw her in your Gastown gallery." When he continued, it was in response to the arching of her left eyebrow. "An old mentor is retiring, and I wanted something special to give him. He's an avid yachtsman, and Christian assured me there was nothing more fitting than one of your scrimshaw pieces. So, I selected this marvelous walrus tusk— *The Marimet Rounding Cape Horn.*"

Melissa was well-acquainted with the piece since it was one of her personal favorites. But, then at one time or another, all of her works were. She'd long ago decided she was either going to do her scrimshaw as a hobby, in which case she could feel free to hoard all her favorites, or as a business, where everything was up for grabs. Well, maybe, not everything. She'd become so

fond of *the Neputine Brig on the Rocks at Point Hatteras* that it
had gotten no closer to sale than the harewood console table in
her study. "I'm surprised Carol didn't mention you'd stopped
by."

"Oh, I didn't tell her that I was your doctor. I thought she'd
take that as some kind of hint for a discount. I gave her cash and
used only my first name."

"Too bad you didn't ask for that discount." Melissa gave
him the kind of look that said he was free to take what she said
next as gospel or joke. "It would have given me an opening to
ask you for a discount for *your* services."

"Didn't Christian tell you your treatment and his are on the
house? I owe him more than a few."

"How hard I argue depends upon the talk I have with my
insurance man. If he balks at my posh accommodations,
maybe, I can make up the difference by giving you some
scrimshaw. In the meantime, I *will* tell Carol to see you get a
double discount on anything that might immediately catch your
fancy."

"Could you be sure she gets the word by today, noon?"

"You remember something you liked?"

"You mean besides Carol?"

Melissa was going to warn him that Carol was taken by
Kevin, but she didn't get the chance.

"We're having lunch today," John said. He misread her
surprised expression. "I promise to be on my very best
behavior."

Melissa tried to remember the last time Carol had lunched
with a customer in off the street, and couldn't. Of course,
Melissa spent a good many hours on the road, traveling between
her Vancouver, Seattle, and Carmel galleries which left a lot of
Carol's lunches unobserved.

"I'm seriously considering buying another scrimshaw piece
that Carol almost sold me. Beautiful!"

Melissa wasn't sure if he referred to Carol or to the piece of scrimshaw.

Had she misinterpreted Carol and Kevin's relationship all of these months? Faulty deductive reasoning based on circumstantial evidence was a disease that seemed to be making the rounds lately. She had to admit, when she thought about it, that Carol and she never really shared the nitty-gritty of their lives outside the work place. Therefore, Melissa had no real basis for her assumptions other than the general feeling that had always prevailed.

Apparently oblivious to Melissa's curiosity about Carol's romances, John examined her aches and pains. Finished, he said, "I'm a firm believer that people mend faster out of hospitals than in them. If you're *really* up to it. I see no reason why you shouldn't be home. Just how steady are you on your feet?"

"A bit wobbly," she admitted.

"But not so much that the first policeman to see you on the streets is going to pick you up as falling-down drunk?"

"Not nearly as wobbly as all that."

"Then, I'll have your discharge papers ready at the front desk when you are. And be sure to keep with whatever the physical regimen you've established over the years, because, from a purely medical standpoint, you are in fantastically good shape to be where you are after all you've been through."

She hadn't figured on such an easily managed escape. "You're serious about my being able to go?"

"Not that I wouldn't welcome you sticking around."

"Not today!"

John did have one more surprise up his sleeve before leaving. "I'm the one who sent a team to recover Elizabeth Howard's lost meteorite before she could get back for it."

"You?"

"Elizabeth and the colonel blamed Christian, right?"

"Right?"

"Well, they were way off base! I knew how badly Christian wanted that rock, and I knew where it was supposed to be, because I quizzed him while I examined him. My lawyer quoted 'Rights of Salvage.' He didn't know whether any of it would stand up in court, but he did know possession was nine-tenths of the law. Professor Telegreen, from the California Institute of Technology, flew up to take charge. He's devoted a lifetime to known meteor impact structures around the world. After spending two days looking for this one, he called the search a lost cause."

Melissa sighed with relief. "The meteorite Christian now has is *really* from Nova Scotia, then?"

"He had someone working out of Halifax who'd tracked rumors of this one for months. It just so happened, he found it the same time Elizabeth lucked onto hers a whole continent away. Word reached his office to say the package was on its way the very day the news broke that you and he were missing. It was waiting for him when he checked out of the clinic. A too good to be true coincidence? What it was was about time!"

"But when Elizabeth asked to see it, he refused."

"I suspect, it was the way she demanded, not asked, in front of all those reporters, and the way she appeared to be foaming at the mouth. Christian figured he didn't owe her, or her U.S. army colonel any favors. They wanted to try and disprove his proof-of-purchase documents, say they were forgeries that he had cooked up on a couple-days notice. They were free to give it a college try."

"I suspect that once Elizabeth got a good look at it, she would have realized her mistake and quit making such a fuss. If that's the case, Christian really wasn't being as fair as he could."

"Well, don't you suppose one stony-iron meteorite can look pretty much like any other? Anything that survived that trip over those falls could have come out of the wash looking far differently than when it was dropped in. Christian could just hear Elizabeth screaming, 'Foul!', No matter what."

"What if Colonel Sampson hears how you were behind the search of the crash site while Christian was under your care? That could persuade him that something might have been found to warrant Christian forging documents to disguise its real identity. Personally, I can't imagine someone of Professor Telegreen's apparent status having been in Canada for two or more days without someone leaking something. All it would take is one slip of the tongue for the colonel to start nosing around."

John shrugged. "One of those bridges to cross when we get to it. In the meantime, I thought you might like to know Christian adamantly disapproved of my little project when he found out. Had we returned with the meteorite, I'm sure he would have insisted we turn it over to Elizabeth. He has a very high-minded sense of fair play."

Her breakfast arrived.

"Do you have someone picking you up?" John asked.

"Carol."

"Just don't keep her out past noon. She has a lunch date."

When Melissa called her, Carol wasn't at the gallery. She'd gotten sick the night before and had asked Cynthia to open. Funny, she hadn't notified John, but maybe she hoped for a miracle cure by lunch time.

Melissa dialed Carol's apartment but got no answer. She was about to try the gallery again when Inspector Dwighton called. "Our killer was Geoffrey C. Clamer, Jr., a gung-ho U.S.-Army type who never adjusted to life after Nam. Evidently, he drifted north for our drug scene. Forensics say he 'shot up' just prior to hitting your room, and *that* was the probable cause of Colonel Sampson getting the best of him. All we have to do now is make the connection with Colonel Sampson—some little grudge-spawning incident along the way

—and we've got it made. Open and shut, although I would like your statement for the file. How about if I stop by about three this afternoon?"

She gave him her address.

She gave the cab driver the same. In no time, wearing the change of clothes and carrying the vanity case Carol had brought to the clinic, Melissa was in front of her apartment building.

It was GREAT to be home!

She headed up the walkway as the car pulled up across the street.

"Melissa?"

She turned back. "Carol?"

"Can we talk?" Carol looked bad as she stretched to open the door on the passenger side. She had dark circles under her eyes. She had a line of discolor along her right cheekbone. A bruise?

Something was wrong. "Carol?" Melissa slid in beside her.

"I'm sorry, Melissa." She started to cry. "He made me."

"He?"

"I wouldn't look back to identify the 'he' in question, Miss Jordan." The voice was low, no-nonsense male, and it came from the back seat. "Doing so might find you prematurely dying."

"I don't know who he is or what he wants." Carol's tears were coming faster. Unsuccessfully, she tried to wipe them away on the back of her hand. "He grabbed me after I left the hospital yesterday."

"We'll have plenty of talk-time, later," the voice guaranteed. When she glanced up, Melissa saw nothing reflected in the rearview mirror.

"Are you the invisible man?"

Carol's look warned against humor.

"Temporarily invisible in my crouch down here on the floor,

as is my gun, as are my bullets that will go right through the seat of this car, Miss Jordan. Right through you and Carol like a hot knife through soft butter. So get your act together real fast. Miss Westingham?"

Carol eased the car away from the curb.

Nausea and fear welled up inside Melissa.

4

The car crossed Lion's Gate Bridge and veered toward Horseshoe Bay.

"Just what is it you want?" Melissa managed to choke out. She still had nothing of their kidnapper but his threatening, disembodied voice.

"Why don't you guess?" he said.

"I haven't the foggiest idea."

"Maybe if I give you more time."

"*I* have been thinking!" Carol injected. "I've been thinking and thinking and *thinking!*"

"Well, both of you think a little harder! Try any revelations that might have come your way quite recently."

Melissa calculated her chances of opening the door and dropping on the pavement. She'd probably die from the fall, or be run over by the car behind them. What if she just banged on the window and yelled, "Help!" to the next passing motorist! Whoever saw her would probably think she was crazy. The madman would shoot her and count on Carol to maneuver them safely through traffic.

"Why don't you give us a hint?" she suggested.

"You're going to get all sorts of clues in good time. You can bet if you know something that I'll find it out, too. I'm handling things, this time around, not that hop-head Clamer."

"Geoffrey Clamer?" The fist in Melissa's stomach clenched tighter.

"Clamer?" Carol was bordering on hysteria. "I don't know any Clamer."

"He was a magician known for firing bullets into a roomful of people but only killing one. Want to tell us how he managed that slight of hand, Miss Jordan?"

"What does that have to do with Carol and me? Clamer had it in for Colonel Sampson . . ."

"Who's Colonel Sampson?" Carol interrupted. "Won't somebody *please* tell me what this is about?"

"He's a U.S. military advisor attached to CanTech." Melissa tried to make her voice soothing. "He and Elizabeth Howard were in my hospital room when Clamer walked in with a machine gun and started firing."

"Noooooo!" Carol was obviously exhausted and near the breaking point.

"It was in anticipation of just such an emotional reaction that kept me from telling her that disturbing news, Miss Jordan. She's distraught as it is."

"You better not have hurt her!" Melissa's anger almost gave her the courage to turn around.

"She's fine, aren't you, Carol? Carol? Tell Miss Jordan—or, maybe I'll call her Melissa, since we're all going to be very chummy before all of this is over."

"I'm fine, Melissa. Really." She didn't look fine. She didn't sound fine. She didn't act fine.

"Look, Clamer had something against Colonel Sampson,

right?" The available pieces of this puzzle didn't fit. "Something war-related. Maybe, thv colonel gave the order that got one of Clamer's buddies killed."

"Yes, and maybe you should rethink that bit of cockamamie," he suggested.

"So, why *did* he gun down Sampson?"

"It was my understanding he gunned down Elizabeth Howard."

"She was unluckily in the room."

"Actually, both she and Sampson were unluckily in the room."

Melissa's blood ran cold. She knew what he insinuated, but there was no way she'd believe it. It didn't make sense.

"In the end, no harm done, since he covered his mess by dying. I should have done it this way in the first place, but I got a little excited, you know? I should never get nervous, because it always plugs my pipeline to them."

"Them?"

"Nothing about which you need concern yourself."

"Can't we discuss this face-to-face?"

"He's got a ski mask." There was a tick at the corner of Carol's left eye. "He's worn it from the start."

"I'll show myself in a bit." It didn't sound like something to which Melissa should look forward.

"Who was Clamer there to kill!" Melissa persisted.

"We'll talk later."

"He had no reason to kill *me*."

"Oh?" He was frustratingly noncommittal.

"Why would he want to kill me?"

"Why would *I* want to kidnap you?"

"Can't you give a straight answer?"

"I don't *have* to give anything, *dear* Melissa." She didn't like the way he said it. She didn't like anything about him, and she didn't need any more than his voice to confirm it.

"May I remind you there are laws against kidnapping in this country?"

"I want you to shut up, Melissa. You're becoming so b-o-r-i-n-g!"

He sounded crazy, and fear rose again in Melissa's throat. She tried to push away the fear that clouded her mind, so she could think, form a plan to escape.

"Melissa!" Carol flicked dank hair out of her eyes.

What *had* their kidnapper done to Carol? There was that glazed look in her eyes and the deepening rainbow hues along her right cheekbone. "You hit her?" This added to the horror of their situation.

"Carol knows what befalls those who don't respond quickly enough to my politer requests."

Melissa didn't answer.

She attempted to focus on how to escape; but she didn't see many favorable options. "Why two lunatics in my life in less than twenty-four hours?" Unbidden, it slipped out.

"I'm keeping a running tab, Melissa, of everything you say that I don't appreciate. I'm going to recall them to you when it comes time for dues-paying." He chuckled. "I can easily handle some poor soul so recently out of her hospital bed."

She regretted not following through on the self-defense classes started by a friend, Jenny Sinclair. Lack of time had made her drop out, plus the dangerous mentality that nothing could happen to her; she was too careful and too much on her toes. Well, she'd certainly walked into this fast enough.

If Melissa could only get to him. She'd attended enough of Jenny's classes to go for his eyes, his Adam's apple, his instep, his . . . Unlike bullets, though, she didn't have access through the seat between them.

Could she wait until he came out of his hole and made the mistake of getting a little too close to someone he assumed drained by her experiences of the last few days? She hadn't come through all she had to let him bully her into playing sick games.

"You *do* remember where you're going, Carol?" Even out of sight, he obviously kept track. "Scheduled for a left turn, aren't we?"

"Just up here. Really." Carol sounded fearful that he wouldn't believe her.

There was a service station up there, too. Melissa wondered what would happen if Carol just pulled in and stopped? The attendant was in front; so was the driver of the car getting gas. There was another guy at the vending machine. Three men: six strong arms ready to take on this man who had overstepped civilized boundaries.

Melissa willed Carol to put them into that service station. Faced with three witnesses, the madman wouldn't blow her or Carol away.

In the end, her conjecture was moot. Carol didn't turn into the station but onto a dirt road.

"Exactly where are we going?" Melissa was less confident now that they'd left the main road. She didn't like this road because she had no idea what was at the other end or anywhere in between.

One of the publicized advantages of living in Vancouver, now a decided disadvantage, was how quickly civilization gave way to wilderness. Walk blindfolded for six feet to any side of this road, strip off the mask, and *try* to guess in which direction, less than an hour away, exists the city of over one million people.

"He has a cabin." It was another indication Carol wasn't completely without a will of her own.

He wasn't pleased to see it. "Consider that a debit for your side of the final accounting sheet."

Carol shivered; Melissa shivered along with her.

But she was determined *not* to let this get her down. Not an easy resolution, considering all that had gone on.

"There are people wondering where Carol and I are."

He wasn't impressed. "So?"

He came up out of his crouch with a suddenness that filled the rear-view mirror with his ski-masked face and completely filled the car with his malevolence. "Trick or treat!" His laugh was animal-like, devoid of humor.

His eyes peered from a face otherwise concealed: ebony eyes, predatory eyes, unforgettable eyes. Give Melissa a hundred men, and she'd know this one by his eyes. Did he know how they betrayed him, made his mask superfluous wrapping?

He looked not fat but well-built. Maybe, though, that was an illusion. How big, after all, was the area he filled back there? It was important she keep her perspective so she could give the authorities an accurate description.

He held up his right hand so what he held replaced his face in the mirror. "G-U-N, gun": an adult warned a two year old. He, then, shifted gears: "Beretta M51. Manufacturer: Pietro Berreta (Italy). Ring any bells: Pietro Perrata?" There was tension in the woof of the fabric stretched across his mouth. Was he smiling? "Here's a hint: Model-12 s.m.g."

"I know nothing about guns." She did know she didn't like them. She didn't have one in her house, although that might change if she ever got out of this.

"It might behoove you to remember this gun fires eight rounds. We've progressed beyond six-shooter status."

"You're a weapons expert?" She wanted more to tell the police.

"He prefers knives." Carol's knuckles were white on the wheel. Her lips were taut. Her eyes were focused straight ahead. Her forehead and upper lip were beaded with sweat.

Melissa wasn't fond of knives, either. Except for the utilitarian cutlery in her kitchen, she owned only pieces from her father's collection: knives with his exquisite workmanship on the handles.

"Now, Carol!" he warned, but this time, she chose to ignore him.

"Don't you like knives?" she challenged.

"Knife or gun: both kill."

"My father made knives." Melissa tried to draw him out.

"Your father made knife *handles*." It was a fine distinction Melissa had made many times. How ironic to have it thrown back at her now! Did his knowing the distinction tell her something?

"You've heard of Charlie Jordan, then?" Keep him talking. Pinpoint the man, behind the words and the mask.

"Oh, yes. In fact, I'm sure since you're his daughter, you can enjoy the nuances of this delicious coincidence."

"What coincidence?"

"Plenty of time to probe it later. Perhaps, it will amuse you before . . ." He let it drop.

"Did anyone ever tell you it's impolite to leave sentences unfinished?"

"I think, Melissa, you may find your sentence ending too soon to suit you." He was all concealed smirk.

She sensed duplicity of meaning, and Carol confirmed, "He's going to kill us, Melissa!"

He came forward with a swiftness that spawned unbridled fear, and he grabbed a large handful of Carol's hair. He shoved the barrel of his gun into her neck at the base of her jaw. He commanded, "Stop the car!" All the while, he fixed lifeless, reptilian eyes on Melissa. "And *you* stay put, or I'll blow her head off."

The car, stopped where it was, would draw attention from anyone passing in either direction, but there was no traffic. There was nothing but the car, two women, a madman with a gun, and a forest of parenthesizing trees.

"Ladies, game time *is* over!" He kept his eyes on Melissa but jabbed his gun deeper into the vulnerable flesh of Carol's neck. "You either tell me now what Kevin told you, or else you tell me where I can find him so I can ask him myself."

"Kevin?" Melissa's surprise was gross understatement. "Kevin *Silner?* This has something to do with him?"

Carol said something, but the position of the gun scrambled the sounds. The gunman translated, "She says Kevin told her nothing. She's said it so often, I'm inclined to believe the lady doeth protest too much."

He released his death-hold and withdrew into the back.

Without waiting to be told, Carol put the car in gear and started off.

"Maybe he told you nothing," he conceded. "Then again . . ." Lest Melissa comment upon yet another open-ended sentence, he waved his pistol back and forth, like a metronome, and completed his statement. ". . . maybe he's told you a lot. Either way, I promise you, I will know eventually."

"He's crazy, Melissa!" Carol's voice was a hoarse whisper. Her left hand massaged her gun-damaged throat. She steered the car into a side road better designed for a horse-drawn wagon.

Melissa didn't need Carol to confirm his unbalanced mind.

The car proceeded slowly, deeper into forest. Gloom cast by the surrounding trees made Melissa all the more uneasy. Nor was the dilapidated cabin conducive to good cheer.

"Looks deceive," he said when the car stopped. "Its basement is quite livable, isn't it, Carol?"

"If you're a mole."

"Let's pretend we're moles."

"Why would a snake like you want to pretend he's a mole?" It had simply been too good for Melissa to pass up.

He ignored her and dropped his free hand over the top of the seat; Melissa's first thought was to grab hold and bite, but then she realized his other hand held the gun. "First, the car keys, please."

Carol handed them over.

He got out; forcing them to follow.

"You won't get away with this!" Melissa didn't want to go into this cabin with this man. She was afraid she was going to die in this place.

"You'd be surprised how much I've gotten away with already."

Not now she wouldn't

His gun waved Carol into the lead, and it was obvious she'd been there before. She went around one side and entered the cabin through a section of collapsed wall. She knelt and pulled up the trapdoor to the cellar. Automatically, a light came on to illuminate the stairway that disappeared into the depths. Carol shivered, and Melissa gave her a reassuring hug.

"Did I ever tell you how much easier it is to interrogate friends?" His eyes remained hard and cold as stone.

"I'm sorry, Melissa!" Carol's voice broke with sobs.

Melissa tightened her hug. "Everything is going to be fine." Unfortunately, not even she believed it.

The stairway was steep; Carol, familiar with it, reached the bottom first. Melissa was not only unfamiliar with the lay of the land but in no hurry to explore it; so she followed slowly.

When a phone rang unexpectedly somewhere below, the kidnapper was apparently anxious to get it, and he gave Melissa a shove to hurry her along. In her windmilling for balance, she caught hold of his arm which he'd reflexively, undoubtedly to his eternal chagrin, reached out to steady her. For a split second, his gun was on her right shoulder not in her back.

Maintaining her hold on his arm, she bent forward, squatted, and pulled him over the top of her in a somersault. Jenny Sinclair would have been proud.

Carol got out of the way as he landed unceremoniously at her feet, and his gun skittered under a heavy workbench where neither he, Carol, nor Melissa had ready access.

Down, but not out, he grabbed Carol's ankle as she stepped over him on her way up the stairs. She went down with a thud scraping her knees and banging her chin.

Melissa grabbed Carol's frantically extended arms, and, collapsing onto the step behind her, gave a tug that, had the man's hold been more solid, would have dislocated Carol's arms at her shoulders. Carol was wrenched free, and neither woman stuck around for any attempts at disabling a man already exhibiting superhuman powers of recovery. They went up the stairs and out. Carol dropped the trapdoor shut behind them.

When she was out of the cabin and in the woods, Melissa's legs buckled. Carol immediately stopped to help her.

The car was left behind, useless without keys, hot-wiring it was impossible, since they had neither the expertise nor time.

The forest had hiding places and they targeted it for safety. Melissa had survived in it and could survive in it again.

There were, however, limits to her energy reserves, even when they were supplemented by Carol's willing and eager assistance. "I'm done!" Her gasps for breath were ragged punctuations. "You go!"

"Can you make it at least as far as that dead log? I'll help."

"Help yourself! I'll hide when I'm able."

"Listen!"

Melissa literally stopped breathing to do that. Otherwise, her rasping pants were all she would have heard.

Birds, wind, and water sounds didn't count.

"Nothing?" Melissa made it a question.

"And that's all wrong, isn't it?"

Melissa liked thinking he hadn't bothered following or that he hadn't recovered from his fall, but she didn't buy either one.

"I'll take a look," Carol said but looked as if it were a questionable idea.

It was then Melissa saw the cuts for the first time; they were revealed by the way Carol's blouse had come open in front. She reached out to those striations on white flesh, but she didn't touch them. "Carol, for heaven's sake!"

Almost embarrassedly, Carol fastened two buttons; the third was missing. "He likes knives," she said. "He likes cutting with them."

Carol left Melissa alone with that nightmare vision that jabbed itself like an icy fist to her stomach. But while what she'd seen made her sick, it gave her the spurt of adrenaline to conceal herself behind the log. She lay there and consciously recruited energy to replace her depleted reserve. Her mind played what if . . . the telephone hadn't rung . . . she hadn't been so cautious on the stairs . . . he found her here?

"Melissa?" Carol was back with a curious expression on her tired face. "He's left."

"No!" Melissa emphasized with a shake of her head. She didn't believe it for a minute. Not for a second or any fraction thereof.

"I circled back to the cabin. He came out, got in the car, drove away."

"He's out to get us up the way, then, or he's headed for the service station where he knows we'll try to make a call. The man may be crazy, but he's not stupid."

But was there a closer, more convenient phone?

Carol dashed her hopes: "He took the phone with him." She dispelled visions of console and handset ripped out of the wall: "It was one of those phones in cars, only in a briefcase."

"I had no real desire to go back, anyway."

Carol's shudder said it better, as did her knife cuts again visible through a pucker of blouse material.

"Let's move!" Melissa got to her feet.

"How do you feel?"

Melissa marveled at how Carol could be concerned about her when she'd been tortured by a madman. Melissa would have been embarrassed to say anything but, "I'm fine."

But they expected to find him behind every tree every step of the way. No sign of him was almost worse than some sign.

It was night when they spotted the lone service station through the last of the trees between then and the highway. It was open, its attendant, paperback book in hand, behind plate-glass windows. The phone booth was an isolated beacon of hope that could as well be a trap to ensnare.

They waited until there were two cars in for service. One driver looked like a professional wrestler. The other wasn't nearly as imposing, but there was safety in numbers.

The women approached, far enough apart so their enemy, when — not if — he appeared, couldn't cover them with one gun if they ran for the people at the station and screamed bloody murder all of the way.

They were surprised to reach the booth without incident.

They were suspicious when Melissa pushed open the door. "If I were a gambler, I'd bet it's dead," Melissa said.

"Me, too."

They would have lost the bet: Melissa got a dial tone but didn't have the faintest idea which police force had jurisdiction. Better to let Inspector Dwighton in Vancouver delegate authority. Until then, Melissa needed a reassuring voice. She had the operator dial Christian collect.

"Where on earth?" His concern traveled the line and warmed her. It was the rejuvenation she needed.

She gave him the condensed version and felt, all the while, like a prisoner given one last call. If this were drama, the critics would complain it didn't play right. Because there was no way she and Carol should have been allowed to get this far!

She hung up and joined Carol outside. "John Feaswell was there and he's coming, too." She tried for humor: "He wants to make sure you have a valid reason for standing him up at lunch today."

"John . . . Feaswell?"

"My doctor, your date." She saw the realization dawn. "I want him to look at those knife cuts; they could get infected."

Reflexively, Carol's fingers pinched shut her blouse where it opened at her missing button.

They moved into shadow and across a gully so they could be less easily surprised from the road. They didn't reenter the trees, afraid of what might await them there. They didn't trust the obvious confinement of the station.

They sat among weeds to break up their silhouettes against the tree line.

Carol began helpless sobs, and Melissa wrapped a reassuring arm around her friend. "Do you want to talk?"

It wasn't herself, however, or her horrors with that man about which Carol wanted to talk. "Oh, Melissa, Kevin's my brother."

Which left Melissa dumb-founded. "I didn't know, I didn't know."

"I thought you might have guessed," Carol said, wiping her eyes.

"How could I?" Melissa was at a loss. At the same time, she felt guilty because she probably could have guessed if she'd made the effort. She'd just assumed the two were . . . well . . . Not only had such assumptions always embarrassed her, but they were, she'd conjectured, probably based on things none of her business. "Kevin Silner, Carol Westingham," she said, as if two different names explained and excused her ingnorance.

"Blame Gregory Westingham for the one." Melissa was slow, so Carol helped with, "My husband."

"You're married?" The revelations coming like buckshot made Melissa dizzy.

"Past tense." She blew her nose. "For two months when I was sixteen and he was twenty. Disastrous. Horrible! Probably something I wouldn't have talked about even if you'd asked."

Melissa hadn't asked. Most of her employees had been friends before she'd hired them, or they'd been friends of friends, but Carol was the exception. She'd been chosen purely on the basis of her enthusiasm, her willingness to accept her own artistic talents as mediocre while unselfishly promoting the works of others whose skills she knew to be better then her own.

"My maiden name is Templin," Carol confused even more. "Silner is the new identity Kevin chose after he ran from the VA Hospital in Los Angeles. It took my parents and me six years to find him here under that alias. He still only recognizes us part of the time, only then in private. We've talked to psychiatrists, and they say he's just running from his old self and what that old self had become." Her voice broke. "They haven't a clue when he'll come out of it — if ever."

"Just how serious is his drug problem?" Melissa couldn't help feeling that all of *this* had something to do with *that.*

"Each time he quits, I think it's for good. He always says it's for good. So far, it hasn't been."

"I do want to know one thing, and I do expect a truthful answer.

Carol anticipated: "He's been clean the whole time we've known you."

"You did know I had to ask?" There'd been the time she'd thought Kevin on drugs, and she'd told Carol so. Carol had admitted Kevin had once been on them, during and even after the war, but she'd sworn he was clean at the time. As proof, she'd referred Melissa to Dr. Paul Elander who had assured her that Kevin's disorientation at that moment was a recurring nerve disorder, the aftereffects of a body too long deprived of necessary diet and essential vitamins.

"Mae Ling has really been marvelous for him."

"Mae Ling?"

Carol seemed confused by Melissa's confusion. "Kevin's girl friend."

"Kevin's girl friend?" Melissa felt like a parrot.

"Surely you knew?" She continued. "Her father and brother were addicts in Nam. How she managed with them, how she manages with Kevin when he's like they were, I don't know.

"When Kevin and I were kids, he was fun and full of life. He was a joy. The war took all of that out of him. He came back drained, broken, beaten: a shell of the original man. Three years a prisoner of war: three years! Held eleven months in turkey pens where thousands of birds had been machine-gunned by retreating forces with a Sherman-march-to-the-sea mentality, left to rot, only their bones finally to mock the starving men one day held captive among them.

"There was this local artisan who the Cong accused of collaboration. They broke all of his fingers, then both of his arms. All the while, he kept an awl hidden from them, but not to kill himself. 'Life is too precious!' he could say, even then. He'd grip the awl with the toes of one foot in order to punch filigree into turkey bones he'd hold with the toes of his other foot. 'Beauty is where you choose to find it,' he said, 'even in a boneyard of soon-to-die men and long-dead fowl.' " She sobbed uncontrollably. "Kevin told me that, Melissa; Kevin who does try to find some beauty, even now."

The fast-moving auto veered suddenly off the highway and braked to a squealing stop. Its headlights caught Carol and Melissa in a blinding white glare that hypnotized as securely as the most skittish doe became mesmerized by the illegal spotlights of poachers.

5

Melissa stood, Carol along with her. Tension-taut muscles prepared to send them in different directions; he wouldn't get them both.

Except, he'd brought help: a second large silhouette joined him in the light in front of the car.

"Melissa? Carol?" It sounded like Christian, but hadn't the ski-masked man said looks deceived?

"Christian?"

"Me, too!"

John?

Carol was a spring almost wound too tightly.

"We can't see your faces." Melissa wanted them there, but an inner voice warned that the madman wouldn't allow a happy-ever-after ending.

"Hold on!" The one who was—or wasn't—Christian went back to the car.

"This is a trick!" Carol predicted. She moved farther away

to make sure Melissa and she were even less a combined target.

"Flashlight!" Its shape was an extension of his uplifted arm. He came forward, switched it on, and shined it directly on his face. The other man did, too.

Melissa's flooding relief was a physical thing that danced her feet. "Christian!"

He crossed the gully and took her in his arms. "I'm so very glad to see you!" He kissed her.

She welcomed his lips as much as his arms. He gave her confidence that together they could fight and beat any lunatic!

Carol and John greeted with more constraint. "Carol?" He took her hands in his. Then, sensing her need for more reassuring body contact, his arms enfolded her while she shivered like an abused kitten too long in the rain. "I've hurt you?"

She shook her head. There were tears in her eyes.

He was more specific: *"He* hurt you."

"Yes." She tapped her index finger to her temple. Then, the gist of his question got through. "Oh, here, you mean?" She'd flattened her palms across her blouse. She shivered again and said, as if it somehow made it better, "He never cut very deep."

"We'll take a look," he promised, all professional. "The sooner the better." He turned to Melissa and Christian still locked in a comforting embrace.

Christian answered John's unasked question: "Yes, let's get out of here!"

Melissa and Christian got in front. He looped his arm around her shoulders and pulled her head against his chest; she heard the reassuring, steady beat of his heart.

He backed the car out and headed the way they'd come.

Not a sign of the madman although Carol's nervous glances searched the darkness for him while John made a cursory examination of her wounds.

Eventually, they talked about the kidnapping.

"Thank God, Kevin decided to walk downtown from the hospital after we visited Melissa." Carol could be magnanimous, even though her brother was the cause of whatever she'd endured. "The guy was really upset he only had me to show for his efforts. I suspect, he figured to wipe the slate clean in one fell swoop."

Melissa mentally replayed the conversations in the other car. Would she ever stop? "Does anyone know anything about Pietro Beretta?"

"I think it's a munitions company. Italian?" Christian sounded unsure.

"And a Model-12 s.m.g.?"

"S.m.g.: sub-machine gun?" John sounded as if he were guessing, too.

Melissa, though, thought they'd hit the nail on the head. "Who wants to guess what weapon Clamer used to shoot down Elizabeth when he came gunning for me?"

"We can ask Inspector Dwighton about the ballistics report." Christian gave Melissa a reassuring squeeze. "He's meeting us at your apartment for debriefing, by the way. He said it's better if you're questioned in familiar surroundings, away from reporters prowling the night desk for a story."

"Surprisingly considerate for a cop," John said.

However, their reception was anything but low-key. Headlights from two parked squad cars illustrated the bold black letters stretched on yellow ribbon across the road: **POLICE BARRICADE: DO NOT PASS.** The policeman, immediately at Christian's car, apparently hadn't gotten word they were expected. In no uncertain terms, he told them to move on.

"The lady . . ." John motioned toward Melissa in front. ". . . happens to live up there, and we're all expected by Inspector Dwighton. So, unless you're letting cars through from the other side, we've somewhat of an impasse."

"Lieutenant!" The summoned officer left off talking to a young couple on the sidewalk. "I think we've got that incoming car for Dwighton."

The Lieutenant came over to the car. His associate moved off to tell a group of youngsters to "Move on!"

He leaned down and filled the open window.

"Miss Jordan, Miss Westingham, Mr. Wynard, and Dr. Feaswell," John introduced them.

"I'll take you through." He opened the back door; Carol scooted over to let him in.

"Pretty big fanfare," Christian said. "I understood this was to be handled a bit more discreetly."

Several reporters, like bloodhounds, were at the car, and flashbulbs popped.

"I'm sure Inspector Dwighton will answer your questions," the lieutenant informed them.

A policeman unfastened one end of the bright yellow streamer and let it drop. Several other policeman held the press back until the barrier went up again.

The lieutenant leaned forward when the car reached Melissa's building. "Just stop in the garage access."

"We're not supposed to block the entranceway." Melissa's warning was born of countless condo-resident meetings where that message was constantly drummed home.

"I'm sure it'll be all right this once," the lieutenant assured; Christian brought the auto to an obedient stop.

"Miss Jordan?" greeted the white-haired, gray-eyed man immediately at the front window. He focused on Melissa.

"Inspector Dwighton?" She vaguely remembered him from the hospital.

"A little late for our three o'clock appointment, but I'll take into account the extenuating circumstances." He opened the door and helped her slide out.

"We were expecting a slightly more subdued reception,"

Christian complained not for the first time.

"Yes, well the best laid plans of mice and men . . . and all of that. Would you all be kind enough to come inside?"

Surprisingly, they were not taken to Melissa's condo but to the manager's quarters on the ground floor. He was nowhere in sight, but the number of police made his premises look like a squad room.

Dwighton ushered them through one room and into the quieter dining room where he dismissed the lone policeman at the table. He asked them to sit while he shut the door to isolate them from the ongoing hubbub.

He flipped through paper on a metal clipboard the young policeman had left behind. "What with so much going on, I'm somewhat at a loss as to where to begin. As to your kidnappings, Christian did fill me in over the phone."

"Is there any reason why we can't conduct this at my place?" For Melissa, this scenario rang no more true than their kidnapper letting them go free once they'd temporarily turned the table on him.

"Yes, I suppose why *is* as good a place to begin as any." After more paper shuffling, he said: "Name: Kevin Silner. One-point-eight meters. Approximately seventy-seven, seventy-nine kilograms. Brown eyes. Red hair. Caucasian. Male." He looked up. "A very dead Caucasian male, I might add. Guess where?"

Melissa reached for Carol's hand. She expected hysteria but got none. "Kevin Silner is her brother!" What an inconsiderate lout the inspector was.

"I'm dreadfully sorry!" He sounded it, too. "There's no record of any immediate family."

"One would be hard to come by." Carol, then, asked for a glass of water.

"Yes, of course." The inspector got it himself from the wet bar in one corner.

She drank it all, set the empty glass gingerly on the table, folded her hands behind it. "What am I feeling at the moment? Surprisingly, very little. I've expected this for such a long time that now that its happened it's anticlimactic. I'm sad he's gone. I'll grieve his passing. But he's responsible for a lot of pain and heartbreak and, along with everything else . . ." She shrugged.

"You say you expected this? How exactly?"

"Drugs. What else but drugs? Buying. Selling. Using. Whatever. He's been high most of the time since he came back from Nam, until this last year, there were only a few intermittent periods of non-use sandwiched in between. I saw signs he was starting up again. Such a waste!" Her eyes welled with tears. Inspector Dwighton produced a handkerchief which she took.

"You insinuated he was murdered in my condo!" Melissa was incredulous.

"He told the building manager he was there to water your plants. Something, I take it, he'd done before."

"Once. I went to Europe. Carol was supposed to do it, but she broke her ankle; Kevin filled in."

"There's a rather disjointed message on your answering machine that lets you know he was coming."

Christian spotted the discrepency: "Why call to let her know he was coming if he were setting up a drug deal?"

Dwighton pursed his lips in thought. "Perhaps, he was confused; the recording suggests he was high at the time. Maybe he called merely to make sure she wasn't back from the hospital, her condo empty and convenient."

"Any drugs on the premises?" John wanted to know.

"Several packets. coke: very high-grade: cut only twice. I'm surprised the killer didn't stop to retrieve them, but he might have been short on time. It was the noise that had neighbors call in the complaint. I recognized the address and headed right over. It had to be pretty noisy to penetrate these walls."

There was a knock. Dwighton went over to the door and

came back a couple seconds later.

"I know how difficult this is, but I must ask you ladies to identify the body."

"Carol *and* Melissa?" Christian was protective.

"Confirmation never hurts. As it's Miss Jordan's condo, it would help us if she looked around and gave us any impressions of something missing, something not as it should be. She'd be more effective in offering Miss Westingham moral support than I can, much as I might try."

"Of course." Melissa didn't want to see the body! However, this wasn't something Carol should face alone.

"Thank you." He gave an appreciative nod.

"Does it have to be now, after everything else they've been through?" Christian tried for a delay to make it easier on the women.

"I assure you, it won't get easier."

John interrupted. "I'd really like to get Carol someplace where I could wash and treat her knife wounds."

"Knife wounds?"

"The kidnapper was a knife freak," John said. "The cuts don't appear to be deep, but I'd like a better look at them."

"This man. This knife freak. Can you give me his description?"

"He wore a ski mask with only holes for his eyes," Melissa said.

The inspector went to the door and opened it. "Kingston still here?" he called to the officers.

"He's back out front, inspector!"

"Well, send someone to tell him I want Beth Delaney down here ASAP to take a look at some knife cuts." He turned back to the group at the table. "Ladies? If the gentlemen will excuse us?"

He ushered them into the elevator and pushed "4." When the trip was over, the door opened, they were assaulted by the

distinct aroma of Shalimar perfume; so much an excess of
costly fragrance made Melissa as uneasy as a miser home to find
a trail of pennies leading from his doorstep.

"Are you all right, Miss Jordan?"

"Just a bit dizzy." It took longer than she expected to regain
her equilibrium, although, in total, it wasn't more than a few
seconds; the inspector waited patiently. "It's rather unnerving to
look forward to getting home, and, then, have to face this."

"Yes, I imagine." If he weren't sincere, he was a good actor.

"I'm fine, now," she assured him. Granted, her balance was
restored, but what waited ahead?

"Miss Westingham, how are you managing?"

"As well as can be expected."

Melissa wished Christian were here for moral support.

The smell of Shalimar was overpowering as it oozed from
Melissa's condo. Something had obviously happened to the
bottle of the perfume she kept on her vanity for special
occasions, but this wasn't the kind of special occasion she had in
mind.

"So, this is how death smells?" Carol sounded grateful.

"Check to make sure everyting is ready, Manny," the
inspector said, "We don't want to keep them longer than
necessary."

Manny disappeared inside.

"No murder scene is pleasant," the inspector warned them.
"This one is particularly nasty. If either of you feel faint or sick,
tell me, and we'll sit you down or get you to the restroom. Since
even police aren't immune to these things, the bathroom is
always the first thing we dust for prints and clean for reuse."

"It's okay to take them in." The young officer resumed his
position by the door.

Immediately, Melissa was brought up short by how much of
a mess there was. End tables were overturned, so was one heavy
armchair. Knickknacks from the mantle were scattered on the

floor, several lay broken on the marble hearth. There were streaks and stains on the wall and rug that Melissa chose to ignore.

The inspector stood between the women, a supporting hand for both.

In the study, one leg of her heirloom harewood console was broken off. *The Neputine Brig on the Rocks at Point Hatteras* lay in a corner, the blue plaster on the rug around the whole tooth, and the corresponding gouge in the wall, gave evidence of a violent scenario.

She had an urge to pick it up but remembered the inspector's warning. She was, therefore, surprised when he retrieved it. "Already dusted," he explained and showed her the fine gray residue on the pale yellow enamel. He turned the Leviathan tooth in his fingers. "Beautiful scrimshaw. *Really* fine. One done by you?"

"Yes." She appreciated the praise, but she wanted the task she'd been conscripted to perform over and done with. She took Carol's hand and squeezed; Carol squeezed back.

"I suppose there is a particular style and technique for every artist," the inspector continued. "A piece like this wouldn't even have to be signed, right, and anyone would know it was by Melissa Jordan?"

"Such a person would have to know his artists and his scrimshaw." She resented the small talk.

"One artist, though, can pretty much recognize the work of the competition by something as simple as how the scrimshaw is scratched into the matrix, whether a piece depicts a ship or a horse, whether it's done in black ink or multi-colors." It wasn't a question. He looked for a place to put the tooth down and finally put it on the chair cushion which looked out of place on the nearby floor.

Finally, and Melissa thought long overdue, he led the way to the bedroom where the havoc ended with a curtain torn off its rod, the bedding cascaded off one end of the bed, an original oil hung cock-eyed, and a spilled bottle of Shalimar still leaking heady fragrance into the air.

Kevin lay along one wall, covered by several sheets.

Inspector Dwighton knelt beside the body. Melissa moved closer to Carol and wrapped an arm securely around her. She took a deep breath.

"Yes!" Melissa said when the edge of sheet was pulled to reveal Kevin's face which looked surprisingly peaceful.

"Yes!" Carol confirmed; she and Melissa turned to go.

"I hate to draw this out any further, but if you could give me a moment more."

They turned; he still knelt by the body. Kevin's face was covered, but an ivory knife handle seemed materialized from a swirl of tainted sheets. Its scrimshaw was a long-tailed shooting star arching a dark and brooding, moon-like landscape.

Carol gasped. Her hands went to her blouse and fanned over the cuts beneath. "*He* did it!" she accused.

"He?"

"He used that very knife to cut me."

"You're sure?"

She challenged: "Do you think I could *ever* forget?"

"No; you're quite right."

"Someone told him where he could find Kevin. Someone phoned. That's why he didn't come after us."

"Miss Jordan?"

Melissa's look of abject disbelief wasn't entirely the result of Carol's surprising revelation.

6

"That knife is one of five blades made by Kyle Wynard and 'hilted' by my father over ten years ago," Melissa said, feeling more in control as long as she kept talking. "It was one of two knives made from two meteorites found on my father's wilderness property in the fifties. My father gave both meteorites to Kyle Wynard who melted them down for the iron content in order to convert them into steel blades. Both knives became part of Kyle Wynard's permanent and personal collection."

"A man who collected his own knives? Doesn't one usually collect the works of others?"

"Some do," Melissa said with a shrug. "Maybe they can't create satisfactory beauty of their own. Maybe they can create beauty but haven't the resources to hold on to it."

"You think knives beautiful?"

"I think many knives, including most of those by Kyle Wynard, can be considered verifiable works of art, yes."

"But deadly pieces of art."

"Using an ashtray to kill someone doesn't make it less an ashtray." She wondered if the analogy fit. If not, it was more satisfying than calling upon the hackneyed, "Knives don't kill, people do."

"That collection of Mr. Wynard—the elder—was stolen, Wynard brutally murdered by the thief?"

"Yes, and the knife that killed Kevin is one of those that was stolen as part of that collection."

"Neither the killer nor the collection ever found?"

"Not unless you know something I don't."

"Strange how a knife, its blade by the father of the man you crashed with, its handle by your father, in possession of someone who kidnapped you and Miss Westingham, ends up killing a man in your condo."

"You think you're going to hear me argue the point?"

"You're sure about the knife?"

"Easy enough to verify." She went to the closet but was stopped by traces of gray dust still on the mirrored doors.

"Go ahead," he said.

She opened the closet and pointed toward a cardboard box on the top shelf. "In there."

"Ah!" If he didn't know what was in the box, he'd make the effort. He stood on his tiptoes and dislodged what Melissa had needed a stool to put up there.

"It's my father's old files." She knelt and began shifting through folders she hadn't seen for years.

"Is it true your father learned scrimshaw from an Eskimo who sailed the whalers out of Kadiak?" He strained for fleeting glimpses of the photographs of Charlie Jordan's work that appeared as Melissa shuffled paper.

"From *the son* of an Eskimo who used to sail the whalers out of Kadiak," she corrected. "Chuteni Icebear was not as fond of the open sea as his father. Hated it. Preferred the woods. My dad had his property up north then; Chuteni helped with odd jobs and sold his scrimshaw on the side. One thing led to another . . . Ah!"

She pulled the photograph and handed it over.

"Yes," the inspector confirmed its resemblance to the murder weapon.

"Are you going to need me much longer?" Carol looked and sounded exhausted.

"She should really get those cuts looked after." Melissa had been so involved she'd locked Carol and Kevin's body out of her mind.

"Forgive me!" He took Carol's arm and led her to a chair. He eased her into it.

"You're not through with me." It wasn't sarcasm, merely her weary statement of assumed fact.

"A short minute more." He went around the bed to the answering machine. "If I could ask you both to . . ." He paused. "I do believe I've rewound it too far."

He turned it on.

". . . not at the hospital, not at the gallery, but not at home, either? John, I suspect, won't approve. Neither do I." It was Christian's voice. "I'll call you later, and you'd better be full-tilt into recuperation."

There were two more messages, each from a more concerned Christian, before the inspector got what he wanted.

No voice; not at first. Only distant music; some stringed instrument played in a *chromatic* scale. The name of the instrument escaped Melissa: something from China or Japan that conjured short-lived images of teahouses and geishas soon replaced by images of opium dens or some equally nefarious equivalent.

"Oh, yes, that's Kevin." Carol was certain even before her brother's breathless voice materialized.

"Melissa? Melissa? Melissa?"

"He does sound as if he's on something."

"Oh, yes!" Carol agreed. "And he's listening to that old, worn-out phonograph record brought back from Nam.'"

"Melissa." Dreamy. Disembodied. "We have to talk. Important. Interesting. Very interesting. Dangerous. Possibly very dangerous."

"Tell me about it!" Carol injected.

"Too dangerous to lay on Carol," Kevin said. "Too dangerous to lay on you, but I think you should know."

There was a short, dissonant, musical interlude.

"I wanted to tell you at the hospital, but the colonel with the old hag scared the you-know-what out of me," Kevin came on again. "Major heart attack time. Bad vibes. Sweats. Flashes. Shakes. Want you to understand. Maybe you can figure."

"I told him there was no way you'd understand if he went back on drugs," Carol risked the inspector's displeasure to say. "I told him he would blow it all; you wouldn't sell his work if you thought his profits went to support his dope habit. Would he listen?"

A wave of the inspector's hand warned Kevin was due again.

"I'll come tonight, Melissa." He'd come and was dead on the floor because of it. It was strange to listen to his voice and see the sheet-covered body that once was he. Oh, Kevin, what was it all about? What was worth dying for? "Tonight. Tonight.": sung to a tune from *West Side Story*. It was so sad that Melissa wanted to cry. Carol *did* cry, her face buried in her hands.

"Please! That's enough," Melissa begged. "This day has been a nightmare and on top of everything else, we don't need this."

"Six o'clock," Kevin said and the line went dead.

"And dead by six-fifteen," said the inspector.

"The man who killed him is certifiable crazy, take my word for it," Melissa said. The scent of Shalimar was stifling and Melissa knew the smell would forever conjure images of this scene.

"Well, that's pretty much all I have." He helped Carol up. They retraced their way to the elevator; Carol leaned against the wall, eyes shut; Melissa wanted to go to bed and sleep for days.

The inspector asked: "Do either of you know why Kevin would use his last breath to say something that sounded like, 'Beatty forgot we had same teacher!'?"

Carol shook her head, and Melissa said, "Sure that wasn't E.T., rather than Beatty?"

"E.T.? Tell me, please, that we're not talking the little green being from the Spielberg movie."

"Kevin came back for a few minutes at the hospital after Carol left and before Elizabeth and Colonel Sampson arrived. He insisted we needed to talk—about E.T."

"You're joking!"

"Cross my heart."

The astonished expression on the inspector's face was short-lived and quickly returned to deadpan. "Kevin have a history of visits from little green people?"

"When he was high on drugs, he could have visits from the Jolly Green Giant, or the Cabbage that Ate Cleveland," Carol volunteered. "You want answers, contact Mae Ling."

"Kevin's girl friend." Melissa informed him.

"And where would I find Mae Ling?"

Carol shrugged. "Every time I saw her she was at Kevin's place. I thought she lived with him."

They exited the elevator and returned to the manager's condo.

Christian greeted them with, "Finally!" He hugged Melissa and asked Carol, "Are you okay?"

"Exhausted and drained are adjectives that immediately come to mind." She looked for a chair.

The inspector spotted, "Sgt. Delaney!"

Model-thin Beth Delaney had gray-streaked auburn hair.

Her black-streaked green eyes took in everyone at a glance but revealed no judgments. "Kingston said you wanted me."

"Miss Westingham," he put his hand gently on Carol's arm, "has some knife cuts I'd like you to see. If she, you, and Dr. Feaswell," he nodded toward John, "could find someplace with a little privacy."

"I could do this far better at my clinic." John's patience seemed in short supply.

"Humor me." The inspector turned to Melissa and Christian; Beth took Carol in tow and John, none too happy, followed. The inspector handed the photograph to Christian. "Miss Jordan tells me this is a picture of a project completed by your fathers."

"Yes," Christian nodded.

"So sure, so fast?"

"Yes."

"Your father had many knives in his collection. It must be difficult to pinpoint one on cue."

"Not this one. Its steel was derived from meteorite iron. I'm interested in crafting my own meteorite knife these days, in case you hadn't heard."

"It's the murder weapon." Melissa tried to read the expression on his face; but it eluded her.

"Not only that, but it's the knife the kidnapper used on Miss Westingham. What, if anything, do you make of that, except that we suddenly have a good idea how the killer got in?"

"My keys!" It had dawned on Melissa that her keys, brought to her in the hospital by Carol, had been lost in the shuffle.

"I think you're right," the inspector said.

"I think you should contact the Los Angeles police department." Christian handed back the photo.

"LAPD? Really?" The inspector's eyebrows arched. "Why?"

"Because this isn't the first knife from my father's stolen

collection to be involved in a homicide."

"Oh?" Christian certainly had his attention.

"Ask for Detective Paolo Sanchez. He was up here a couple of years ago to have me identify a knife connected to the murder of some woman, or, rather, several women, in the L.A. area."

"Could you be more specific?"

"He was rather vague, but I don't doubt you could get more out of him. He seemed concerned he might let go specifics of an ongoing case to someone with no need to know."

"I believe I will check with him. Any more surprises?"

"The knife in L.A. was from meteorite, too." Which surprised both the inspector and Melissa.

The inspector found words first. "From the second meteorite down on Jordan land in the fifties and handed over to your father by Charlie Jordan?"

"No. From one down in Baja, Mexico, in the twenties. It was what first got Dad hung up on his meteorite-to-knife interests."

"This case gets curiouser and curiouser, to coin a phrase."

"There's a killer out there with a penchant for knives made from meteorites," Melissa concluded.

The inspector took her arm and moved her closer to the wall; Christian unwilling to release Melissa came along. "We certainly do *not* want to jump to *that* hasty conclusion." His voice was low to a whisper.

"Why not?" Christian asked. He'd thought her conclusion very apt.

"Imagine what a field day the press would have with *E.T. Killer* or *Death Weapons from the Moon*. We'd have banner headlines on every supermarket tabloid from here to Timbuktu. Have you ever tried to conduct a police investigation with every UFO fanatic within six-thousand miles tumbling out of the woodwork to follow your every footstep and hang on your every move? Besides, I seriously doubt the killer, if there is only the one, has a penchant for knives made *only* of meteorites."

"I disagree!" Christian vehemently championed Melissa's suggestion. This made her suspect something more than mere chivalry, but she couldn't put her finger on what.

"How many knives in your father's stolen collection?" The inspector was good at this. "One-hundred-fifty? One-hundred-sixty?"

"One-sixty."

"All from meteorites?"

"Of course not."

"Why scoop up the needless excess when all he wanted were three?"

Melissa, not pleased with the inspector's smug attitude, said, "He didn't want us to see the trees for the forest. He didn't want us labeling him Killer from Outer Space."

"Exactly!" Christian agreed.

The inspector disagreed. "More likely, he picked the murder weapons at random from those available."

"Do you know the odds against that?"

Melissa read the inspector's fear that the tabloids would get hold of the story and run with it.

"The assumption has been made here that the killer, one day, decided to commit a few murders with *only* knives made from meteorite, for which purpose he stole three such knives." The inspector was obviously trying to make what he had to say as clear as possible. "When one knife got lost in L.A., he used knife two which he has now lost here. But not to worry, he still has knife three in backup."

"Maybe not *just* knife three."

The inspector didn't follow him and neither did Melissa. "There were more in your father's collection?"

"There was one in the Dailinty collection, one in the Freeburg collection, one in the Masner collection: all three collections were stolen over the last few years, gone underground without a trace."

Information so specific hadn't likely come off the top of his head. For the first time, Melissa had an inkling of why Christian had probably been scrounging the Canadian wilderness for a bit of stony-iron dropped from the sky to use in making a knife of his own; her blood ran cold.

"Coincidence!" The inspector wasn't going to be carried by argument.

What had her kidnapper said about coincidence and how Melissa, Charlie Jordan's daughter, might find "their" coincidence particularly amusing? The coincidence that the man who killed Christian's father for murder weapons, now was forced to kill Melissa for something Kevin had told her? Drugs and knives? The hair stood up on the back of her neck. Gooseflesh covered the entire surface of her legs and arms.

"The way *I* see this," the inspector continued, "the killer never chose meteorite knives specifically. In fact, he's probably killed more times, with more different knives, than we'll ever know. It's a pure fluke that the two knives he was forced to leave behind turn out to be from meteorites. Until that's proved different, I want you two to keep your outer-space theories under wraps."

They were interrupted by the return of Beth Delaney, Carol, and John; the latter looked anything but happy.

He demanded, "What exactly does this policewoman mean by, 'These definitely fit *his* m.o.!' "

Noise in the room stopped. If looks could kill, Beth Delaney would be impaled from several different directions as securely as any collector's pins ever skewered butterflies to corkboard.

"Let's talk in the dining room," the inspector insisted.

"Here, the dining room, or in your superior's office, I intend to have an answer," John said.

The inspector led the way. At the door, he dismissed Beth with a cool, "I'll talk to you later." He closed the door and turned to four determined faces. "I was telling Mr. Wynard and Miss Jordan about repercussions from leaks to the press which obstruct police investigations." He raised his hand to keep John silent. "What has, unfortunately, occurred here is as much my fault as it is Delaney's, because I didn't brief her to your status as attending physician."

"You've seen cuts like Carol's before." Melissa felt it obvious. "Where?"

"I'm sure we would all be very sorry to cause any further emotional distress to either you or Miss Westingham, Miss Jordan."

"Where?" Carol and Melissa asked in unison.

"Three women to be precise," the inspector capitulated. "Maybe a fourth, except her remains are too decomposed to tell."

"Her remains?" John sounded as if he wished this particular can of worms had been left unopened.

Melissa now knew why the inspector was so grateful for the tip about the knife murders in L.A.

"So, why haven't these murders been reported in the paper?" John said, insinuating he read every conceivable news source.

"They were, but only briefly. They were not prominent women; in fact, they were at the complete opposite end of the spectrum. We purposely chose to downplay their deaths because of certain sensationalistic aspects which, like killers from outer space . . ." John didn't catch the reference, but the others did. ". . . could do more harm than good for our ongoing investigation."

"I knew he planned to kill us," Carol said with conviction. "His eyes said it."

"Neither Carol nor Melissa fit his modus operandi as a choice of victim," Christian observed. "Melissa: well-known gallery owner and artist. Carol: her employee. Hardly your typical no-one-to-notice murder victims."

"I suspect he was prepared to be flexible within a situation forced on him."

There was a knock, and the inspector went to answer it. He spoke in a low voice that Melissa couldn't hear.

"A bit of interesting news," he announced shortly. "Kevin's phone was bugged. Not with penny-ante stuff, either. Top-grade, U.S.-government issue. Expensive, but then, there's lots of drug money floating around these days especially with the big boys."

"Kevin was never involved with the big boys," Carol disagreed. "Strictly small potatoes."

"The killer knew where Kevin was, then, because he had someone monitor Kevin's phone?" Melissa wanted to be sure.

"Monitor *and* record. There's a tape of Kevin's conversation with your answering machine. Which should make you ladies sleep more securely tonight."

"How do you figure?" Christian challenged his assertions.

"Melissa," the inspector said, "why don't you explain what's on the machine?"

"Kevin admitted he hadn't told Carol or me anything. He wanted me to know; that's what he was doing here."

"So the killer knows Kevin didn't reveal anything during his stopover with Carol to visit Melissa at the hospital."

"And since Melissa and Carol don't fit his m.o. as victims, he's through with them?" John didn't sound convinced.

"Crazies can be surprisingly consistent when it comes right down to their preferences for murder." The inspector sounded as if he should know.

"You don't think this little incident might have slipped him out of his rut?" Christian was no more convinced than John.

"How great his compulsion to kill them if he let them go?"

"He didn't exactly *let* us go," Melissa reminded them.

"He didn't give chase, then," he corrected. "Think about it: he had his man on Kevin's phone to report in the minute Kevin showed; the guy calls the killer; the killer goes after Kevin when, had he really been hot to kill you two, he needed only to tell his man to keep Kevin in view while he took care of two bits of unfinished business. So much easier to track you both in the middle of the woods than wait until you're plopped down back here among family and friends, spilling what you know, to the likes of me."

"Why aren't I comforted by such superb logic?" Melissa asked.

"For the same reason I'm not," Carol said.

"You're all tired! You'd all like to get a good night's rest. I'm going to let you go — for now. Provided you remember nothing said here goes any farther."

"Go?" Melissa exclaimed. "I live here!"

John, though, was way ahead of her. "The clinic has a penthouse just over on Pacific for visiting V.I.P.s. You and Carol can stay there."

Melissa was tired, and it sounded closer and better than a hotel.

"Oh, inspector?" Christian asked on the way out. "Was the weapon used in the Elizabeth Howard shooting a Model-12 submachine gun made by Pietro Berreta (Italy)?"

"As a matter of fact, it was." The inspector looked startled.

"How do you suppose our kidnapper knew that?" For Melissa, that was one piece that had finally clicked into place.

"Maybe it means we should call off the search for someone with a grudge against Colonel Sampson," the inspector said.

It was only minutes to the V.I.P. accommodations atop the new condo complex. Two-story windows looked out over English Bay to the dim lights of freighters skimming the horizon. To the right were the nighttime lakes and trees of Stanley Park. Outside looked peaceful; inside seemed safe.

"And if relatives of some clinic patient fly in from Saudi Arabia?" Melissa asked after John's prefunctory tour of upstairs and down; he produced the phone numbers of twenty-four hour housekeeping service and the hotel restaurant next door that provided meals.

"Unexpected arrivals get the back-up condo down on Beach."

"I should phone my parents," Carol said. "I'd prefer they get the news from me."

"Why don't you use the phone in there?" John pointed toward privacy in a downstairs bedroom.

"I've a call, too," Christian requested. "I presume this comes complete with more than one outside line for the usual brand of clientele who needs more than one broker at a time?"

"Try the phone in the master bedroom."

Melissa slipped off her shoes and sank into a leather chair that immediately molded to her contours as if made for them. On the adjacent phone, one light, then another, glowed with the outgoing calls. "What, I wonder, is the term for *beyond* bushed?"

One phone light went out; Christian came down the stairs. "I presume we should now exit."

"I thought I'd give Carol a sedative when she was through."

"Tonight, all I need for sleep is my head against a pillow."

The other light went out, but Carol didn't return to the room. Melissa found her on the bed, the phone on the bedspread beside her. She had tears in her eyes and must have found it difficult to speak, because she nodded when Melissa asked if she wanted something to help her sleep.

Melissa rejoined Christian. Tempted by another collapse into the chair, she chose Christian's supportive arms instead. They made her feel safe from all the machinations of the killer. What they'd been through together the last week had forged a bond that Melissa doubted could ever be broken. The attraction was still present, but there was a depth to her feelings beyond just the physical. She knew that she could depend on him no matter what the crisis. Right now she was so weary that she felt extremely vulnerable and her guard was down.

"You and I have to talk," she said, enjoying his little kisses around her ear. "I've things to say that should be said when I've cleared away the cobwebs."

"Things about us?" He pulled back slightly and she could see how pleased he was from his expression.

"Among other things." Unfortunately, there were confrontational aspects she didn't want until she was fresh enough to handle them.

"You feel it, too." He kissed her cheek. "This magic between us."

"Don't try to take advantage of my sorry state to pry anything from me now that I won't be prepared to back up in a more lucid state. Just promise we can talk first thing tomorrow."

"Why don't you call me when you feel like company?" His smile said he really doubted she'd be up before noon.

John emerged from the bedroom. "She'll sleep through until morning."

Melissa walked them to the door where she allowed herself a parting kiss from this man who was starting to mean so much to her. Leaning against the closed door, she was tired enough to fall asleep right there. The on-again, off-again spurts of energy required by the day and those preceding it had drained her dry. She had just enough strength to reach the downstairs bedroom. In a less exhausted state, she might have tried for the more luxurious appointments of the master bedroom.

Not even a bath. Just the big bed, and . . .

She thought it was the front door buzzer; John or Christian might have left something behind. On the third buzz, she realized it was the telephone.

"Forget something?" The resulting long pause told her she'd missed her bet. "I'm sorry, can I help you?"

"Melissa Jordan, please." There was a pleasant sing-song quality to the woman's voice.

"This is she."

"It's important I see you, Miss Jordan. My name is Mae Ling."

Melissa's eyes came open. She tried to organize her thoughts. "Do you know what's happened to Kevin, Mae Ling?"

"That's why I'm calling."

"How did you know I was here?"

A very cryptic: "Friends."

When no further insight was forthcoming, Melissa emphasized, "You should contact Inspector Dwighton. There's the possibility you may be in danger."

"More than possibility."

"Call the inspector!" Melissa had questions that Dwighton was better qualified to ask.

"Kevin warned me about phones." There followed a pause so long Melissa almost filled it. "I did not believe him, of course. I thought it was the drugs talking."

"If his killer even *thinks* you know anything . . ."

"Kevin said you had power to see silk purses in sows' ears, to sell his work which he once was embarrassed to give away. He left something for you that you should have before I leave the city."

"Leave Vancouver?"

"It's a question of this killer. It's a case of the police who may not understand certain irregularities surrounding my arrival in Canada."

Melissa saw information on the verge of evaporation. "When do we talk? Where?"

"It must be now or never." Melissa's groan was silent, but Mae Ling must have sensed its reverberations. "I know the inconvenience. You have been through much lately, but I can't linger where the killer might easily find me."

"Yes, I understand."

"There is a shopping mall a few blocks from you. Do you know the one on which they've built pink condos. It has three theaters, a row of pay phones near Theater One."

"I know it."

"In fifteen minutes, one of those phones will ring." No time, then, for a taxi. She would have to walk. She was tired but still dressed. "You will receive further instructions there."

Someone spoke staccato, Oriental language in the background.

"It would be unwise to bring anyone with you, especially his sister," Mae Ling resumed. "Kevin was most insistent Carol not be involved."

The line went dead.

She went to tell Carol, but Carol was asleep. She scribbled a note. She grabbed the keys.

The private elevator emerged into a small lobby all its own. A locked door separated it and Melissa from the outside.

It was dark out there, and she wasn't sure she wanted to leave the cocoon of safety she'd found here. How did she know it had been Mae Ling? It could have been any woman, paid by any man, to say any thing.

Resolutely, she pushed open the door. She refused to be held captive of her own fears. She wouldn't be shackled by *what if* . . . he's really out there; he's laying traps; he's out to finish what he started. She couldn't—she wouldn't—live that way!

She was reassured when, two blocks on, she saw people on the sidewalk with her who looked as if they belonged there. Many Vancouver residential neighborhoods, this one included, coexisted within business districts. Evening walks took whole families by store windows that, in other cities, would have seen no foot traffic until morning. Occasional shops stayed open to cater to the night crowds. Melissa passed a flower shop where a young man bought his girl friend a nosegay of deep-purple violets.

By the time she reached the mall, there were even more people, and the smell of hot buttered popcorn was heavy in the air. Short-skirted girls flirted with teenage boys. Someone laughed. Someone gave change and two chocolate ice-cream cones for a five-dollar bill.

Although expected, the ringing of the telephone startled her. More startling was the unexpected, angry voice already speaking by the time she got the receiver to her ear. "You said you would come alone! Why did you lie?"

"Mae Ling?" she asked a dial tone.

She put the phone back and turned to confront a world less inviting than she'd just seen it seconds before. Fine hair raised on her arms and at the base of her neck.

What could Mae Ling see but Melissa couldn't? Something. Melissa could now feel it, too: a crawling inside her: not alone, not alone, not alone.

"Mae Ling, which of these seemingly innocuous people is other than he or she seems?"

Two girls looked. Did they think she talked to them? Was one of them named Mae Ling? Did they think her crazy?

She was not crazy, not without recourse, either. Few people were attacked in this part of Vancouver; residents took pride in their fear-free streets; they wanted it safe for their kids to go and return from corner stores at all hours of the day or night. Melissa could call Christian, or John, even Inspector Dwighton. She hadn't brought any money, but she could persuade the operator a call — particularly to the police — was important. But, what did she tell Christian, John, or Dwighton? "I'm here in this shopping mall, people all around, and I'm afraid to walk the few blocks back to the penthouse because a Vietnamese woman, over the phone, said I'm being followed."

Melissa refused to succumb to fear. She'd dumped a

madman over her head and down a flight of stairs; survived a crash landing, a waterfall, bears, a machine gun, a kidnapping. She could survive this, too.

She headed for the door and tried to pinpoint who was interested.

A laughing boy and girl followed her, then turned and walked in the opposite direction.

She walked in the guise of any other local resident out for a stroll. The night was surprisingly warm, without a hint of the more customary chill, drizzle, or mist that would have made it more horror-movie. Street lights showed all nooks and crannies.

Why so much darker, though, as she approached her building? It hadn't seemed nearly so gloomy on her way out when she'd had the brighter lights ahead of her, rather than behind.

She walked faster and heard footsteps behind her. She hurried to escape them, down the sidewalk, through the shrubs and to the closed glass door that separated her from the private elevator in the private lobby.

Keys! She found them while, behind her, the footsteps went on without her. It was someone, like her, on the way home. Not a killer.

She took two deep breaths and tried the key. It wouldn't fit. She tried again, then realized she attempted to force the elevator key into the lobby lock.

As she changed keys, she saw only his legs in the bushes not three feet from her.

7

An enemy located was an enemy more easily dealt with than
one creeping around on the sly. It allowed for strategy that took
into account direction of attack.

While Melissa continued the chore of putting right key to
right lock, she recalled all she could of Jenny Sinclair's self-
defense class.

The lock released; Melissa steeled herself for the inevitable.
He'd take her now while assuming she had a false sense of
security. When he did no such thing, she decided he'd wait to
use the door as a battering-ram to fell her.

When she was not only allowed to step inside but lock the
door behind her, her heart raced like that of a horse around a
track one too many times. She was confused and made hyper by
adrenaline.

She looked back through the glass. The angle showed
nothing but hedge, but instinct told her he was still there. Why?
It was more difficult for him now.

A gun? The barrier was less sufficient in the face of speeding bullets.

Whatever, it was suspect.

She walked to the elevator and shook so badly she needed both hands to direct that key to its lock.

"Now, or never, buster!" she said as the elevator opened and
. . .

She stepped inside. The door shut, and the elevator moved up.

She didn't understand. The odds had always been in his favor.

She collapsed against the wall. She was so weak, what kind of a fight would she have put up after her initial adrenaline-pumped high had deflated with attempted self-defense?

The elevator stopped, the door slid open.

Melissa stayed put and saw the penthouse looking just as she'd left it. The lights were on; the drapes were opened on an outside darkness.

Was someone there, waiting?

How could he have known where she was? Same way Mae Ling had known, obviously. Several policemen had heard John announce where he was taking them, anyone of whom might have knowingly or unknowingly passed on the information.

When the elevator door began to shut, Melissa envisioned him downstairs, summoning the car with her in it. Though, even as she lunged for the "open" button, she could tell neither she nor her container was going anywhere; the shutting was the result of pure design aesthetics that demanded the doors shut when the elevator was dormant for a certain time.

To be sure, she pressed the button that locked the elevator at the top, and she stepped out of it.

The penthouse continued to look quiet enough, harmless enough, but there were plenty of hiding places in it for monsters.

She made sure Carol was all right. Then, she methodically checked the other two bedrooms, three bathrooms, living room, kitchen, dining room, and den on the first floor.

Headed for the stairs, she was distracted by the now-familiar buzz of the telephone.

She didn't even get to say hello.

"Melissa!"

"Christian?" She'd expected Mae Ling.

"Is something wrong?" Was he psychic?

"I think there may be somebody in the apartment."

"How?" He didn't sound convinced.

"I got a call from Kevin's girl friend to meet her in a mall down the street."

"That's why you were out?"

"You knew?" Obviously, he had more than ESP working for him!

"I made arrangements before I left the penthouse — remember my call? — for two men to watch your building."

"*You* have two men following me?" She sank to the floor in a heap, telephone in hand. Even she recognized her giggles as borderline hysteria.

"I know what the inspector said about you and Carol not fitting the killer's m.o., but I decided I'd sleep better if someone watched you this evening."

She tried to control her giggles. She didn't like feeling and acting so uncharacteristically giddy. "You might have said something."

"I didn't know how you'd feel about baby-sitters."

"So, we now have one more thing to talk about in the morning." She wouldn't berate him for fouling up whatever Mae Ling had to give her. She refused to fault good intentions. "If it were reported I was acting erratic, it was because I spotted one of your men spying from the bushes."

"I'm sorry." He sounded it, too. "They're supposed to be

discreet professionals."

"Well, that major trauma out of my life, I'm going to bed."
Her heart still beat as if it recycled her blood supply every ten
seconds. "I suggest you do the same."

Which didn't mean she skipped giving the upstairs a once-
over after she'd hung up. While up there, she drew back the
sable bedspread on the dura-king bed and passed out in the
master bedroom.

The next morning, she woke up with enough of her wits to
wish she hadn't crawled between white satin sheets without a
bath first. Determined to rectify that oversight, she made a
beeline for the bathroom which could have doubled as a
seraglio.

Her reflection, bounced from parenthesizing mirrors, made
her wonder why more people hadn't stared aghast the night
before. Her looks weren't improved by hair she'd obviously laid
on wrong during the night.

She selected pink and green bath salts from a rainbow
selection in mammoth hypothecary jars that took up most of
one wall. When snowy white bubbles rode rising water in the
white-streaked pink marble tub, she headed downstairs to check
Carol.

The note, propped at the end of the spiral banister: You're
sleeping soundly. I'm out to take care of funeral arrangements.
Christian called to say let him know when you're ready for that
talk. Cynthia's opened the gallery. Try the Canadian-bacon
omelet from the hotel restaurant. Thanks for being there for
me. See you later. Carol.

For the next hour, Melissa indulged Arabian Night fantasies
amid hot, soapy water that became more therapeutic when
jacuzzi jets were activated to massage her sore spots and turn
her deliciously supple.

While the tub emptied, she stood in rinsing spray that
blasted her from three different directions.

She wrapped in a thick-nap, terry-cloth robe, taking Carol's suggestion to order omelet. While she had the hotel switchboard on the line, she asked for one of their boutiques and made arrangements for a selection of dresses to be sent over, anything she bought to be billed to her Gastown gallery.

She'd eaten the last of her meal and had decided upon a light-blue wool skirt and light-blue silk blouse when Christian called.

"Feeling better?"

"Much better, thank-you."

"Our talk still on?"

"When can you be here?"

"Two minutes."

"Do us both a favor and make it an hour."

Thank heaven the clerk had enough savvy to have brought along fresh pantyhose; Melissa's were a maze of runs.

She'd looked better in her time, but Christian had seen her look worse. He was gracious enough to appreciate the improvement. "Absolutely gorgeous!"

After accepting both his compliment and his kiss, she ushered him into the living room and onto a couch where she joined him. She settled in for what she hoped would be mutual enlightenment. "Now, where to begin?"

"How about with Mae Ling?"

She obliged.

"Sorry about the boys screwing up that one," he apologized when she finished.

"While on that subject, would you give them their walking papers before the cure becomes worse than the disease?"

"I already have. However, I'd rest better . . ."

"I won't live my life in a world patrolled on a twenty-four hour basis by watchdogs, human or canine. If the killer wants me badly enough, he'll have the intelligence to spot bodyguards and schedule accordingly."

"Whatever." He didn't look or sound pleased, although he'd anticipated just this.

"That over, we now have a few minutes in which you can explain to me how, when, and why you decided to trap the man who killed your father; may have killed women in Los Angeles, here, and who-only-knows-where; not to mention murdered Kevin Silner. You see, I've guessed what you're up to."

She thought he'd deny it, and she feared where that would put their relationship. She couldn't care for someone if there wasn't trust, and their evolving feelings were not the least of what they had to sort out.

"Let me try to put it in perspective," he said finally.

Melissa felt an easing of anxiety.

"One of my first memories of my father is of him home from a hard day and relaxing in his shed out back. For him, relaxing was to stoke up the forge, heat a piece of metal, and hammer away."

His eyes got a faraway look. When they focused on Melissa, she was willingly lost in their magic.

"He would have been a blacksmith in some other time."

She was acutely aware, without breaking eye contact, of his Adam's apple, moving within the satiny column of his muscular neck.

"He would have been a blacksmith in *his* time if it hadn't been for his father who wanted more for his son than what the old shipfitter had known on the docks of Brighton."

He put his elbows on his knees and looked at the floor.

"My dad ended up, until his father died, a glorified paper pusher. He had the big conglomerate, the big money, the big position, the big office, the big car. But, in his opinion, he never had it all until after his father died, and he remodeled one of the outbuildings. He moved in Willy Thompson, a blacksmith from Lillooet, who stayed two years, teaching him his craft."

He got up.

"One day, dad decided to make a knife. Why a knife? He said he woke up that morning to find all the horses in the world already had more shoes than my mother." He smiled at the memory.

Melissa found she wanted to know all about his mother. She wanted to know the rest about his father. She wanted to know everything about Christian as a child, as an adolescent, as a man. She wanted to know his likes and dislikes, his favorite authors, his favorite colors, his favorite foods, whether he cried in sad movies.

"There was no *Blade* magazine in those days. Knife-makers James Wincoe, Steven Crant, Terry 'The Bowie' Sloan — were few and far between. No 'how-to'books, a person learned by doing. Dad's first knife was so ugly . . ."

Melissa interpreted his pause as her cue for some humor. "How ugly was it?"

"So ugly, my mother, for as long as she lived, wouldn't have it in the house," he said absently. "So ugly, my father's killer left only it and the murder weapon when he took the rest of the collection."

Melissa's chill went all of the way to the bone. As she rubbed her arms vigorously to erase the gooseflesh, she resented his shattering something enjoyable.

"You're angry." He sounded surprised.

"Why should I be angry?" She'd refocused her disappointment on herself for having been carried away to some kind of never-never land. He was right to bring things back into clear focus; she'd needed the jarring.

"I'd steal in to watch dad amid all those sounds of ringing metal. His shed was an alchemist's lair, moreso than the stereotype with beakers, test tubes, mortar and pestle. Gleaming blades emerged from dull ingots, like streamlined butterflies from clunky cocoons. I wanted to perform the magic, too, but, at first, I was too young. Then, I had to learn the basics that never produced anything exciting. The basics down pat, I detoured to other interests: cars, girls, sports, school, a career focused on aquaculture, sculpture as a hobby, not necessarily in that order. It was suddenly dad always asking, 'Make that knife today, will we, Christian?', while I was off to do something else."

"A knife never to be made by the two of you." It slipped out: a certain something that hung there, to be plucked out of the air.

"A free-lance writer came around awhile back to interview me for an article he was doing for *Blade*.

"His piece was on all the great knives which had been stolen over the last few years. By great, he meant big-money: the Jilian dagger with the Kerton emerald in its hilt; the Samslinton dirk out of that fancy platinum alloy. A couple of dad's stolen knives, each with an estimated worth of sixty-thousand dollars on today's market, *just* squeezed into his dollar range of interest. He had a lot of the inventories he'd personally amassed of other stolen collections, and I happened to get a glance at them.

"Probably because of dad's intense interest in knives from meteorites, what struck me immediately was how so many of those individual meteorite knives had been included within collections that had been stolen. Someone without my interest might not have been struck by that statistic, because it's admittedly very easy to lose any one group of knives, even that novelty group, among the total stolen.

"Even someone with my interest wasn't likely ever to access such a comprehensive compilation of listed-stolen knives, not even in *Blade*.

"Neither the police, nor any other law-enforcement agency, has any linkup, computer or otherwise, to print out a complete list of knives stolen in Miami, in Toronto, in Seattle, in Vancouver, and anywhere else."

He sat down, took her hand and held it. There was hardly a break in his explanation, even as he brought her fingers to his lips and gently kissed them.

"It struck me how either several thieves now had, between them, a good deal of all meteorite knives ever crafted in North America, or one thief, with a fetish for meteorite knives, had that whole collection to himself. The latter theory allowed me the plan, which you've obviously guessed, whereby, by crafting a meteorite knife and offering it as bait, I might catch my father's killer. I got out the word I was actively searching for a meteorite, old or new, in order to make a knife out of it. Soon, thereafter, I leeched onto another bit of information that seemed to confirm I was on the right track: the next collection stolen, the Blendale collection in Chicago, included a Tillson-designed blade made of . . ."

"Meteorite." Melissa knew it hadn't taken a genius mentality to complete the sentence.

He lovingly linked the fingers of her hand with his.

"Detective Sanchez's visit from L.A. warned me I might be out to nab a psychopath, in the bargain, but it, also, bolstered my conviction that meteorite knives were what this guy was all about. And I couldn't let him get away with it." He paused again and looked her directly in the eyes. "All that's happened lately only makes it more likely."

"You don't think you'd be better off with the police in on this with you?" Melissa asked over a series of flesh-crawling chills.

"The police had their chance, and they came up with nothing. Even having the murder weapon in L.A. didn't get results. I doubt the murder weapon here is going to do them any better. Besides, you heard Dwighton's fears about *Cops After Outer-Space Killer.*"

"You don't find it inconsistent that a killer, who supposedly specifically steals meteorite knives for killing, used a less exotic knife to kill your father?"

"The way I figure it, he wasn't *planning* to kill my father. Dad wasn't due back for hours. The guy picked up the first knife available. It was of so little interest to him, in the end, he just left it; not because dad put up a struggle that wouldn't let the killer make off with it in time; but, *only* because it wasn't what the killer/thief had come for, and he already had plenty of other knives in the Wynard collection to mask his theft of the only three knives he thought genuinely important."

"Be forewarned, you haven't heard the last from me arguing for you to bring in Inspector Dwighton. Until then, what do you make of Colonel Sampson's claim it was a bomb on board our ill-fated helicopter, not an act of God, that caused it and us to go down?"

"What do you mean, a bomb?" He was genuinely taken back by the shift in conversation.

"There's evidence there might even have been more than one."

"What evidence?"

"They found a shrapnel pattern and powder burns on the body of the pilot."

"I don't believe it!" He was convinced Colonel Sampson's source was in error. "Who and/or why would anyone booby-trap that chopper?" He devined the one possible answer and would have none of it. "Me?" It came out impressively loud and laden with incredulity.

"Bad English!" she said, deflating some of the tension.

"Sampson thinks *I* planted a bomb?" He wasn't won over by her attempted levity.

"He and Elizabeth both."

"They said that, did they?" An ugly expression crossed his face. Something Melissa found distressingly ominous, since she'd always assumed nothing was capable of metamorphosing his incredibly good looks into anything so foreboding. "I'll have him up on charges of slander with malicious intent. I'll sue him from here to this side of next Tuesday!"

Quickly, Melissa attempted to recall her conversation with Elizabeth and the colonel. Unfortunately, what immediately came to mind was the colonel saying they weren't *officially* accusing Christian of anything. Would that denial matter, considering what else he'd said? What if he denied saying anyting? What if *he* sued *Melissa* for slander with malicious intent?

"He'll only deny they ever said it," she reminded. "It'll be his word against mine."

"And what exactly was it you were doing all this time they were painting me as the mad bomber?"

Melissa didn't like the look on his face, or the one in his eyes. On the other hand, he was giving her an opportunity which she could convert to her advantage. "I said that to accuse you of blasting us out of the sky for a hunk of rock was ludicrous." He looked less than impressed by her defense. "I told them only a lunatic would plant a bomb, crawl into a helicopter with it, and risk the explosion and the drop, in terrain that rugged, in weather that lousy."

He looked a bit more pacified. "To which Elizabeth probably replied that he *is* a lunatic!" he correctly surmised.

"They were lying through their teeth, of course." He wasn't just talking about their accusation that *he* blew the helicopter. "*No one* would have reason to blow that thing!"

"The Russians?"

His look said her suggestion laid *her* open for charges of lunacy. "The Russians," he repeated slowly, as if he were prepared to reserve judgment, just in case she wanted to retract what it was she'd said.

"Maybe CanTech isolated some exotic metal from meteorites, and the Russians wanted to screw up, or slow down, that research."

"That notion just popped into your head, unassisted, did it?" It really wasn't a smile on his lips but an unattractive caricature of one.

"Colonel Sampson mentioned exotic metals when I asked him what CanTech and he had to hide."

"Asked him that, straight to his face, did you?" His smile became more real; Melissa felt a slight lessening of the tension.

"He said neither CanTech, the Canadian nor the U.S. governments wanted the press camping on its doorstep for this one, like each had for that flying-saucer hoax a few years back."

"That would be Lab Ten." His smile got wider. "Oh, yes, but I imagine there were all sorts of people worried by the press nosing around during that U.F.O. in the Klondike fiasco. Just think what secrets newsmen have accidently stumbled upon while snooping around such sheer nonsense. And I do suspect CanTech has more than its share of legitimate secrets that it, the Canadian *and* the U.S. governments would prefer be kept under wraps."

He got up and paced the floor. "I don't doubt the colonel's sincerity, in the least, when he says he prefers no publicity blitz on this one; the general public is always keen when they think the government is trying to keep them in the dark about things from outer space.

"Sampson seemed genuinely piqued by Elizabeth's behavior after my news conference. Enough so, it's my guess Elizabeth was just a sore loser that no one quite knew how to make into a good one. Considering her tenure at CanTech, I can see how Sampson might have been out to smooth her ruffled feathers with his little I'm-on-your-side song and dance, but I can't, for the life of me, see him going so far as to conjure up this phony bomb business to help her out."

"Either he's a very good actor, or he didn't have anything to do with the story. I saw his face when he got the call. You want surprise: that, take it from me, was it."

"It does sound as if someone is out there to nail me to the wall." He passed by Melissa's judgment on Sampson's lack of, or abundance of, acting skills. "Getting set up to take the fall for the murder of a U.S. helicopter pilot, and willful destruction of U.S. government property on loan to the Canadian government, is *not* my idea of any good times ahead! You're sure Sampson said a shrapnel pattern and powder burns?"

"Can't you check it out with somebody?"

"I can try; but, the very fact that someone came up with this story says to me that my access to candid medical reports isn't liable to be all that easy. However, I do know one guy moled into the CanTech network who might pull it off."

"You're sure it's not the Russians?" She still wasn't sure she understood why he'd rejected that solution as out of hand.

"Not out to thwart exotic metal leeched by CanTech from meteorites," Christian said. "At least not from any data sources I've been able to access about a universe that comes across composed of the same stuff we've got right here on earth. In meteorites, it's just older. Older doesn't mean better, stronger, or a threat to Soviety security."

"Something to do with the CanTech scientist who defected a few years back, then?" She was grabbing at straws, but a search of her mind for CanTech-related material referenced only that.

"Professor Gerald Kleeve . . . Gleeve . . . or something like that?"

"Something like that," Melissa echoed. It happened while her father was dying, and she was surprised she remembered anything, from those hours, unrelated to her personal tragedy.

"If there's a connection, I can't see it," Christian admitted with a shrug, "but I'm keeping all my options open. If that chopper *were* bombed, and I can't imagine that *was* the case, someone, *besides me,* is responsible. You can take my word for it."

Melissa still foresaw trouble when the colonel got wind of

how John had recruited Professor Telegreen for the failed recovery of the meteorite downed with her and Christian. With nothing to hide, Christian could so easily nip any unpleasantness if he'd just let the colonel see for himself that there was no attempt to pass off one meteorite for another dropped from the sky in 1922 in Nova Scotia.

"Look, Christian." She was determined to try. "Wouldn't it be better, all around, if you just gave the colonel his requested few-minutes access to this meteorite of yours?"

"From what I hear, the colonel isn't exactly in any condition to drop by for a look-see."

"Well, he mentioned he'd let me stand in proxy. I've seen one of the meteorites in question, after all."

"You think that's going to satisfy his U.S.-government highness?"

"Maybe not. But if I confirm your meteorite isn't the one Elizabeth recovered, what possible motive can he argue you had for putting bombs aboard the CanTech helicopter?"

"I'm convinced. Shall we go?"

"Right this minute?" She was delighted by her success, but she'd hardly expected to have to act on it so quickly. Today was crowded with things to be done. She had to make arrangements for picking up some of her things, for finding a permanent place to stay, for getting some money from the bank . . .

"It's now, or never, I'm afraid." Which echoed those words of Mae Ling that reminded her how certain information about Kevin was probably lost to them for good; no point, though, in crying over spilled milk. "I've the meteorite scheduled into the smelter this afternoon for extraction of lead content. The colonel might appreciate hearing how you saw it prior to its reduction to standard ingot."

"Okay." This *was* important, and it coincided with her decision to take it easy. How exhausting could it be to check out a chunk of rock?

"Maybe I can entice you to lunch afterwards? I know this fantastic new restaurant on Granville that serves delectable monks fish."

"You've twisted my arm. Though, I would appreciate a store, first, where I could charge a cheap windbreaker. It does look nice outside, but . . ."

"We both know the unpredictability of Vancouver weather," he finished for her. "Actually, I may have an extra in the trunk of my car."

"In that case, let's go!" She looped his arm and liked the feel of its hard-muscle contours.

She was always "up" on Vancouver days that obliged with a bit of blue sky and sunshine. Lately, they seemed too few and far between to suit her, and she would enjoy getting out into this one; actually, she'd never really gotten over the persistent chill that had set into her bones when she'd been in the woods with Elizabeth.

The landscape shrubbery didn't look nearly as menacing as the night before. The sidewalk and street, in bright daylight, didn't look as if they could harbor any kind of horror, even come nightfall.

"Ahhhhhhh!" she breathed pollution-free air. It *was* good to be alive and well with a man as attractive as Christian by her side. "When the sun is out, there's no other place on earth I'd rather be."

"Than on my arm, you mean?"

"Is that what's called fishing for a compliment?" She waited for him to steer them in the direction of his car. "If so, consider yourself complimented."

Content, he turned left.

She spotted his car two-thirds up the next block. With a spring in her step, she'd thought long gone, she walked the distance in no time.

Christian unlocked the trunk while she stood close by.

"Does this satisfy your sense of high fashion?" He held up the light-blue nylon jacket that couldn't have been better color-coordinated for Melissa's silk and wool ensemble.

Her attention, though, was diverted. Intuition, honed by days of danger, had pulled her focus up the street to the approach of six young men. It wasn't that they resembled some motorcycle gang out to rape and pillage; they were all neatly dressed, two in suits. It wasn't that they were Orientals; Vancouver was a truly international city with the largest west-coast population of Chinese north of San Francisco. What it was was the way all six, formed into columns of two, three across to take up the width of the sidewalk, walked in a coordinated cadence that was almost military.

"Problem?" Christian's attention shifted to join hers.

"I very much doubt it." She had to control a lingering paranoia that could detrimentally run rampant if she gave it half a chance. She couldn't go through life assuming herself the target for each and every person, or group of persons, who struck her as peculiar.

Christian prepared to assuage her fears by putting her safely in the car behind its closed and locked doors, but he was made uneasy by his discovery of three other Oriental youths who approached disconcertingly close from the other direction. "Let's jaywalk!" He slammed the trunk while taking her arm.

"You know, we're probably being silly, don't you?"

"Probably," he agreed. At the same time, she might change her opinion once she realized the other three could sandwich them within nine young men with potential to do harm.

The street was empty of traffic one second, filled with a speeding van the very next. The vehicle had actually taken the corner on two squealing wheels as it barreled down on them with attention-getting speed. At the exact moment, nine young men swarmed Melissa and Christian like ants over two sugar cubes at a picnic.

Melissa, her arms suddenly locked painfully behind her, her face stinging from a hand slapped firmly across her mouth, her eyes wide as the van screeched to a fishtail stop but feet from her, simply couldn't believe this was happening in broad daylight on a sunny Vancouver, B.C., residential street.

8

Looks deceive: once said by a madman to Melissa at a dilapidated cabin in the woods. He should have seen this, because when the well-oiled side door of the van slid open, with its sigh of silk on silk, Melissa thought she and Christian would be tossed in like two bags of garbage.

Wrong! All nine attackers peeled off in a coordinated maneuver that put *them* in the van, one right after the other, Christian and Melissa left behind, as the vehicle sped away as fast as it had arrived.

"What the?" Christian sat in the middle of the road, and he looked like a little boy whose sandbox had disappeared out from under him.

Standing, Melissa was equally disoriented. She wasn't sure how she managed the few steps to offer her hand. She did know his fingers were reassuring and welcome. Not for the first time in the last few days, she had thought herself a goner.

"So, where's the cavalry?" He brushed off the seat of his

trousers.

If he were curious, Melissa was, too. A quick look around didn't show any signs of anything that might have offered the nine attackers a threat.

"It happened so fast!" Melissa had been about to add, "didn't it?", but fast was the *only* explanation for no witnesses; unless everyone preferred running indoors to getting involved.

"The question: *what* happened?" Christian checked his pants and found his wallet. He flipped it open.

Melissa immediately spotted a plethora of cash and gold credit cards. Since she had left the penthouse with nothing more than the clothes on her back, she didn't need to worry about missing anything of value.

"What's that?" He pointed to her midsection; she assumed her blouse was ripped; she was wrong.

"An envelope?" She was surprised to see it tucked in her waistband.

"Don't tell me the Canadian postal system is no longer on strike." Unlike in the U.S., where such strikes by government workers were illegal, the running complaint here was how the Canadian equivalent was *always* off the job; its latest bout of inactivity had extended for over three weeks and showed all indications of becoming violent.

"*Too* good a service." Still holding his hand, she returned to the curb before some totally innocent driver came along and made short work of them.

She leaned against the car to catch her breath and relieve the weight on her still none-too-strong legs. She turned the envelope over.

Melissa: the handwriting said; she recognized it, too. "From Kevin through Mae Ling."

"You're sure?"

"He endorsed the paychecks I wrote him, remember? See the narrow loop of his 'e' and the way he dots his 'i' with a comma. Carol could tell us for sure."

"In the meantime, are you going to open it?"

The envelope had been sealed, the seal broken and refastened with Scotch tape Melissa severed with the edge of a fingernail.

"Maybe we should do this inside the car." He unlocked the door on her side.

Melissa slid in and locked the door behind her. He went around to the driver's side and joined her. She handed him the piece of paper taken from the envelope.

" 'Lenny Sylint,' " he read aloud. "Plus what: his home address in a particularly seedy part of town? And: 'Captain Steven E.T. Miller.' Not written in the same hand. Looks like a woman wrote the first. The latter's lower-case 'e', 'l', 'i', and 'a' match those on the envelope, wouldn't you say?"

He could almost hear her mental gears turning.

"It doesn't make sense," she said.

"I guess they weren't taking any chances that they would be detained, by anyone I had guarding you, to lead the way back to Mae Ling. Not even the two big boys I had on you would have successfully tackled that athletic bunch."

Melissa, though, hadn't referred to method of delivery: "Don't you recognize the second name, without the E.T.? *Captain Steven Miller.*"

"Right!" Revelation dawned. "Our pilot!" Not having been part of the CanTech team, Christian had never really known the pilot's name except as he'd glanced over it in the resulting news articles. Even when he and Melissa had discussed the man's death, they'd referred to him merely as "the pilot."

"Except Kevin saw him alive *after* he supposedly died."

"Kevin told you that?"

"A live 'Captain E.T.': that's what he said the day he made his uncharacteristic appearance at the clinic."

"How did Kevin know Miller?"

"Vietnam?" Melissa said. She didn't know, but that was all that came to mind.

"And E.T. ends up the initials of two middle names? Or, are we talking nicknames, like *Top Gun:* Jorge 'Cisco' Cruz, Denny 'Horse' Selby, Craig 'Stuntman' Cower?"

He reached for the car phone.

"Toby," he said shortly. "Christian. I'd like you to do some digging for me. U.S. Army Captain, name Miller, first name: Steven 'E.T.' Assigned support group CanTech: helicopter pilot . . . That's the one! Another, name Sylint, first name: Lenny. Don't know his affiliations or citizenship. I do have a local address." He read it off. "Finally, a license number, last spotted on a lime-green Volkswagen van." He recited it from memory.

Melissa was impressed. Everything had happened so fast, she hardly remembered green, let alone license number.

He hung up and started the car.

Melissa put the slip of paper back in its envelope. "We should probably turn this over to Inspector Dwighton." She tapped envelope and contents against the back of her hand.

"Why don't we swing by the station as soon as we've checked the meteorite—and had lunch?"

"Not before?" She wasn't sure she approved of him giving his man a head start on the police. On the other hand, the police didn't have a very good track record, and the more input, the better the chance of answers.

"The inspector will have all sorts of questions." He turned left on Hornby. "By the time he's done, the smelter people will have the meteorite in their possession and melted down. We don't want you to miss your peek, do we?" He smiled.

"And lunch?" She smiled back.

"We don't want to risk ptomaine poisoning at the station-house vending machines. Cops may have cast-iron stomachs, but do you and I?"

"I suppose I owe Mae Ling, after all her efforts, a little

leeway before putting the police on her tail," Melissa rationalized. "I wouldn't want her deported for a good deed done."

"Whatever Toby finds, we'll run it by the police," Christian alleviated the last of Melissa's qualms. "An independent, inspired by money, has a little more incentive than police overloaded with so many other crime cases."

She settled back in comfortable leather and marveled at a day already more eventful than expected. Maybe, now, she could count on a few hours respite.

They headed for Burrard Inlet and its harbor facilities. They veered east, and the impressive Pan Pacific Hotel, left on the site of Expo 86, loomed on their left.

The warehouse had nothing to recommend it over the others in its cluster. It didn't sit on the water, but sea and sky were visible as an indivisible line just down the street.

"It's only a short walk."

"I'm feeling great. Really!" Maybe it was the weather. Maybe it was the narrow escape and residual adrenaline. Maybe it was Mae Ling's contribution not lost to the investigaton. Maybe it was Christian. She liked him more and more. She liked how natural it seemed for him to take her arm, or her hand, or wrap her waist with his arm. She enjoyed his voice; his hair stirred by any slight breeze; his eyes, bluer blue than ocean-blue or sky-blue.

There was a large door for trucks, a smaller one for people; both were locked. He opened the latter with a magnetic tape on the plastic card inserted into a provided slot on the wall. The resulting click of disengaging lock was almost inaudible; the door, obviously in need of oil, made up for it with a squeak straight out of fright-night.

Grids of lights, all on, hung from the high ceiling but didn't erase all the deep shadows between stacked cargo ship containers plopped down according to some unrecognizable master plan.

"Shall I start unraveling my skirt, a la Ariadne?" She'd once ruined a perfectly good relationship with classical references that her boyfriend could never quite place.

Christian, though, was up to the challenge. He chuckled and said, "Wish the Minotaur on this Theseus, in this Labyrinth, and we'll both be sorry in the morning." He took her hand along a narrow alley formed by locked storage sheds on one side.

They stopped just short of an unlocked door that warned Christian something wasn't right.

"Out!" His command to Melissa was made more forceful in its hoarse whisper.

His strong fingers turned her like a top.

Something sighed high above, and she looked up to see a huge, spider-web-like cascade.

"Run!" He provided the initiating shove.

She was moving fast when the weighty netting proved itself far less lacy than it looked. It knocked her off her feet and held her. It wasn't web-sticky, but it entangled her nonetheless as she fought to escape it.

At first, she thought the people might be there to give her an assist; she still wasn't sure why or who the modern-day retiarius. It soon became evident, though, that these newcomers, she had thought were brought by her sounds of distress, were the cause of it.

"I need help over here, or he's going to get away!" someone warned.

"Well, I've got all I can handle," a man answered; when Melissa jerked her arm free, and the same man replied, "Quit!", she knew who it was he was so determined to handle.

When her mind first began automatically sorting possibilities, she thought the same gang of nine who'd bullied her that morning was at it again. They'd gotten the warehouse key when they'd waylaid Christian and her; except, Christian hadn't missed the plastic key, and it couldn't have been duplicated on such short access.

Someone was on her legs. She claimed a handful of blonde hair; none of the gang of nine were blondes.

"She's got my hair!"

None of the gang of nine were female.

This was a whole new ball game with an offensive team of all new players.

"He's getting away!"

Melissa wished the same for herself. Unfortunately, she was anchored. Even her satisfaction in pulling the enemy's hair was taken away as, one by one, her fingers were painfully pried open.

"Hit him with something!"

"This isn't the way this was supposed to go!"

"Stop complaining! Get a blindfold on this one before she sees something concrete to tell the cops."

"How do you know she hasn't already!"

"How do we know they both haven't?"

"Are you two going to shut up and get this done, or run with your tails between your legs?"

Melissa would have given anything to see better. It was dark and dismal so close to the hard cement floor. Between cargo crates and storage sheds, all the light seemed miles above. There was only enough of it at her level to distinguish blonde versus brunette, men versus women, nothing more.

"Finally!" exclaimed one of the enemy.

The only hair Melissa's hand now claimed were those it had pulled out by their roots.

"Look, get her tied and blindfolded, then we'll cut her out. I'm losing patience."

Melissa's patience was long-gone. She was tired of getting dumped on, and this latest inexplicable battering was not what the doctor ordered.

Something wrapped her eyes, and she didn't like it.

Her mouth contacted warm flesh, and she bit. Her satisfaction with the resulting wail was short-lived and interrupted by a slap that made her see stars and hear bells.

"Hurt her, Alan, and we'll be in big trouble!"

"You prefer: would you please remove your teeth from my arm?"

"What if somebody hears and . . ."

Good idea, Melissa thought. Her loud scream ended when a large hand clamped tightly over her mouth and nose. Her renewal of frantic struggle was her sudden life-and-death need for air.

"You're smothering her, you idiot!" was the last she heard as the fight drained out of her. She entered a world wherein, although she breathed with great, heaving gasps, she was relegated to a haze made completely dark by the blindfold someone finally got in place.

"Success!"

"I'm going to need a tetanus shot. This bite is bleeding."

"Worry about that later and give me a hand!"

She was blindfolded. She was gagged. She was tied. She was propped against something hard.

Her head ached. Her teeth hurt. Her lungs burned.

She tasted blood. His or hers?

"Let me go!" sounded like something an expert cryptographer couldn't decipher.

"Is Wynard all right?"

That was what Melissa wanted to know, too.

"He's breathing."

"Thank God!"

"You hit him pretty hard."

If he hit him *too* hard, Melissa guaranteed there would . . .

"You *said* to hit him."

"If Roger told you to jump off the Pan Pacific, I suppose

you'd do that, too?"

Melissa had a Roger here. She'd had an Alan earlier. These were amateurs, and she would have preferred pros. There'd been something smooth-flowing about the ballet of the gang of nine. Like now, when people didn't know what they were doing, other people got hurt. If she had her way, there was a Roger and an Alan who would bemoan the day they were born.

She didn't envy a blind woman trying to put meaning to sounds. If the other senses became more acute to compensate for one lost or inhibited, it wasn't a rapid adjustment, because Melissa had a hard time figuring out what was what.

These were grunts, groans, and swearing. There was a thud and squeaking wheels. When all of that was replaced by silence, she knew they were gone. Hopefully, Christian was nearby; although, she didn't hear him, even when she held her breath to concentrate on his life-sounds.

She moved but not far. She was tied to herself and to something solid and immovable. She was, also, tied too tightly. Her struggles had apparently made them think she was Wonder Woman, and, novices as they were, they'd not allowed her adequate circulation; her fingers began to sleep. She wiggled them and her toes to keep her blood circulating.

By the time she heard distant footsteps, her hands were numb and her legs were filled with needle-like pinpricks. She willed those footsteps closer, frankly surprised when they obliged.

They stopped, and someone said, "Not you two again!"

Melissa could have cried her relief. "Inspector Dwighton?" came out decipherable only because he removed her gag.

"What kind of treadmill for disaster are you on?" he asked her.

He removed her blindfold; she spotted Christian being untied by one of the inspector's men. Melissa wanted to get to him but was prevented by knots the inspector hadn't yet figured out.

"Is he all right?" sounded as cottony as her mouth felt.

"I'm okay," Christian responded. "My left leg has fallen asleep is all, and I've a bump on my head."

Melissa's relief was an audible sigh.

"How did you find us?" She didn't relish the alternative.

"Anonymous call. I suspect your assailants weren't playing for keeps."

"What were they playing for?" She was no more sure than she'd been of what the gang of nine had been up to before discovery of their delivery.

"They took the meteorite," Christian informed them.

"Why?" She rubbed her wrists while the inspector worked the ropes at her ankles.

"Why did Elizabeth want it?" Christian asked. "Why does Colonel Sampson want it? Why do I want it? I'm sure there's an answer there somewhere."

She tried her feet. Her legs rebelled and she dropped to her knees onto the net left shredded after her extraction from it.

"Let me give you a hand." The inspector knew where she wanted to go. He helped her to get there and eased her down on the floor beside Christian.

"They hit you on the head." It wasn't a question. Her hand followed his to feel the bump raised on his scalp.

"I think," said the inspector, "one of you should begin at the beginning."

By the end, he had it all.

"Withholding evidence is serious business!" The inspector waved the incriminating envelope in front of their noses in emphasis.

"We weren't withholding evidence," Christian disagreed. "We were *holding* it until Melissa saw the meteorite, and we had lunch. We couldn't be sure if it even was evidence. We still can't."

"Don't try to out-fox a fox!" The inspector had obviously heard similar rationale from the best in the business.

"What if the fox has so many cases he needs all the help he can get?" Melissa said.

"What kind of help are you two to me, trussed up like pigs in a poke? Time spent untying you could better be spent elsewhere."

"Does this mean I should contact my lawyer?" Christian asked.

"It means, Mr. Wynard, I wonder why you, a respectable and successful aquaculturist, already with the perfectly satisfactory hobby of sculpturing, are suddenly interested in making a knife from meteorite at the exact moment there are murders by just such a weapon in my jurisdiction; murders, committed by that very knife in L.A., along with a second murder weapon of similar origin."

"You checked LAPD, then, and he used both knives to kill down there?"

"*Murder Weapons from Outer Space,* as the tabloids might scream?" Melissa said.

"I'm still not buying that, Miss Jordan. Although, it does disturb me that Wynard, here, may be hand-crafting another such meteorite knife to bait the killer of his father."

Obviously, Melissa wasn't the only one around capable of surmising Christian's intentions.

"Are you finished, inspector?" Christian asked. He was now mobile. He pushed himself to his feet and helped Melissa join him. "We're hungry, and you have a missing meteorite to track down."

"Whatever game you're playing, Wynard, let me remind you it's not just your life; although, maybe Miss Jordan may be less concerned for her safety than I am."

"You know where to reach us." Christian offered Melissa his arm for additional support. "In the meantime, I'd appreciate the return of my meteorite as soon as possible."

Their exit was less exuberant than their entrance. The car was where they'd left it, although at this point, Melissa wouldn't have been surprised to find it gone.

"Do you think Colonel Sampson is behind it?" She slumped down in the seat, all the stiffening drained from her body, and wondered if she had enough energy left to go to lunch.

"I don't think Sampson would draw on amateurs with so many professionals at his disposal, do you?"

"Who, then?" she said wearily.

"Find Roger and Alan, and I suspect the others won't be far away. Now, about lunch . . ."

The restaurant was on Granville Island. At one time the island had been an industrial area, but now it was a renovated-eclectic array of theaters, galleries, stores, craft and workshops, along with maritime and public markets, an art college, and restaurants. True to Christian's word, the restaurant served delicious monks fish with butter sauce, fresh green beans, and potatoes au gratin. The accompanying bread was fresh and hot enough to melt the parsley butter.

"I once thought of opening a gallery here," Melissa said, glass of Perrier in hand and genuinely relaxed for the first time since her bath earlier.

"Change your mind?" He eyed her over the rim of his glass, fascinated by what he saw. Rather than pale under pressure, she seemed to glow.

"Quite frankly, I've already expanded to where my regular artists are hard-pressed to keep up with the demand. I guess I'm not prepared to take on additional artists, whose work I don't find special, just to fill expanded shelf space."

"Sounds good to me." He didn't care what she said, as long as she said something. He enjoyed her words melodiously tripping off her tongue. It did for him what great music did: his heart beat faster, his breathing almost stopped in anticipation of the next magical moment.

"He's got it all wrong, you know?"

Christian had missed the transition, too caught up in the pleasure of her voice.

"The inspector." She'd seen his mind wandering and had misinterpreted where it was off to. "When he insinuated you were somehow responsible for bringing me into this. It had very little to do with you. It had a whole lot to do with coincidence."

The madman had been right. She could appreciate the continually revealed nuances of chance.

"He's correct, though, in that my baiting a killer might implicate those around me." Christian looked into her eyes. "Unfortunately, I haven't the willpower to put you at a distance; I tell myself the killer's interest won't peak until I have something a lot nearer completion to offer him."

She finished her Perrier.

"We've been through a lot together, haven't we?"

"You think there might be something more than that to whatever we have between us?"

"Well . . ." Right now she didn't want to analyze too carefully for fear of spoiling the specialness she felt whenever she was with him.

"Have you ever been in love?" His voice was solemn like the answer was the most important information he could possibly receive.

"I don't think I ever have," she said slowly. "Oh there have been men who have been important to me, but when dad died, a one-man, one-woman business, suddenly became a full-time, sink-or-swim, one-woman operation and personal relationships fell by the wayside. What about you?"

"I thought I was twice. In retrospect, I think not."

"Oh?" She was embarrassed when she realized that she sounded as if she were blatantly fishing for something she wanted to hear.

"But I'm beginning to think I'm in love with you."

He fulfilled her wildest expectations.

"What do you think?"

"I think I'm in love with you, too." She could not be anything less than honest. "However," she said, "I'm not a scatterbrained schoolgirl to be carried away on a tidal wave of emotions. I think our feelings warrant a bit more exploration by both of us."

"It wouldn't do either of us any good if we weren't sure of a permanent commitment."

"We've taken a lifetime to reach this point, and we can surely spare whatever additional time to make sure." Even as she spoke the words Melissa knew that deep in her heart she was sure. Even after this short of time, she loved Christian without reservations. And if this additional time allowed their love to grow and develop even more, how much the richer they would both be for it.

"Right!" He reached across the table, took her hands in his, and kissed her fingers.

Once again the touch of his lips sent shimmers of delight cascading through her. "I just wish you weren't so handsome, so charming, so wealthy. It does have a tendency to bowl women over," she said lightly in an attempt to dilute the sensations that filled her body at the realization that he loved her.

"Whoever said you couldn't love a handsome, charming, and wealthy man, or be loved by him in return?" he teased.

"Am I really?" she said softly, "Cinderella isn't a fairy-tale?"

"Naw!" He kissed her hands again; she extended an index finger and traced a line from his cheek to his full, eminently kissable lips.

Momentarily, all the traumas of the last few days disappeared. She stopped trying to answer all the unanswered mysteries that confronted them.

As they walked the romantic waterfront afterwards, Melissa

thought she had never been so happy.

Reality, though, couldn't be put on hold forever. Nor did she want it to be. Whatever the life they carved together, she wanted it from substantial stuff that included the good as well as the bad; otherwise, they risked the sudden, someday shattering of dreams too impossibly ideal to exist except in their imaginations. Love was a vital supplement to their lives just as salt was an enhancing condiment without being an entire meal.

"Wonderful afternoon!" she said and scooted into the car.

Whatever he was going to say was interrupted by the car phone.

Christian answered but said very little until he hung up.

"Toby has located Mr. Lenny Sylint. A man with a very major drug problem who doesn't know Toby at all, doesn't know me either, but did know Kevin Silner, and has heard enough of you from Kevin to be willing to budget *you* a few minutes of his time, if you're game."

She would have preferred holding on to the magic of the afternoon for a bit longer before being thrust back into the nitty-gritty mainstream. Then, she realized the magic they'd just lived would be there forever, preserved in their memories like a rare flower locked in amber.

"By all means, let's hear whatever it is Mr. Sylint has to say." She reached for Christian's hand and squeezed it; she wanted to be sure the sheer wonder of this man was really there, so very close beside her.

Unlike Granville Island, the area they entered had no uniqueness or charm to entice entrepreneurs to renovate so obvious a neglected state of disrepair. Cracked and broken windows displayed unheeded FOR LEASE or FOR SALE signs, behind which bare rooms existed beneath bulbless light sockets. Paint was weathered and peeled. Cement was scarred by ragged chips or flaked like dandruff. Street signs were missing or bent and twisted into pretzel-like designs that simultaneously labeled either of two streets with alternative names. Stop signs, what few there were, boasted bullet holes as much a warning as the KILL PIG COPS! scrawled everywhere in large, spray-paint graffiti.

The building with the address of Lenny Sylint, that Mae Ling had supplied, and to which they'd been summoned by Toby Crescent, was a skeletal remain partially gutted by fire and finished off by vandalism.

"Think Lenny moved?" Melissa hugged herself to keep down her distaste of the neighborhood.

"We'll ask Toby." Christian pointed to where a car was stopped beside the curb.

Melissa looked first to the two teenage kids on the hood of the car, each of whom looked more like hoodlums than Toby. Then, she realized, Christian had referred to the man in corduroy and gray-knit cardigan who pushed free of shadows near the building to head their way.

Christian unlocked the back door, and Toby climbed in.

Melissa guessed him in his late thirties, not strikingly handsome.

"This one, Christian, my man, is going to cost you, since this is not my favorite spot to nose around." His voice was low, easy to take, and not without an edge of teasing that made it all the more listenable. "How, by the way, did you get involved with a loser like Sylint?"

"Is he one of those two?" Christian nodded toward the two kids on the car.

"You should be so lucky!" He had a pleasant laugh that said he'd not become so jaded he couldn't find amusement in everyday life; Melissa decided she liked him. "Those two low-lifes see daylight on occasion. What you're after is a regular mole."

Melissa shivered at the reference, because Carol had described the madman's cellar as more befitting that particular ground-burrowing mammal.

"By the way: Toby, this is Melissa; Melissa, Toby."

"You're sure you want your little chat with Sylint under his conditions, Melissa?" His thick brows could have used discriminative thinning.

"Just what *are* his conditions?" Christian wanted to know.

"Merely that she came to him, not vice versa."

"So, where is he?" Melissa didn't expect an easy answer, and she was right.

"There." He nodded toward the fire-gutted building. "And straight down about three levels."

"You're kidding?"

Melissa could tell from Christian's tone that he knew Toby was dead-serious.

"There's a regular little community of dopers down there, and, like vampires, residents only come out at night to score drugs or find somebody to mug for the cash to score drugs. It's an underground, rabbit-warren maze, dark, where you can't count on any light but what you bring in with you, or on occasional flares for drug melt-downs."

"No chance of Sylint coming out?" Christian liked this even less than he'd expected from Toby's voice over the phone.

"Word is, he got himself a bonanza the other night when he rolled some drunk still holding leftover winnings from a high-stakes poker game. Sylint used the cash to bankroll enough drugs to keep him flying for a long time, and he's squirreled himself in for the duration."

"He's coherent?" To Christian, the situation deteriorated by the minute.

"To hear him tell it, he indulges only to keep the pleasant buzz that eradicates the irritating static of the work-a-day world. You want my opinion: a borderline. He is, though, someone definitely sane enough to think he has something Melissa wants to hear. He knew, without my ever telling him, that I would see her on his doorstep."

"I think we cancel." Christian hadn't counted on Mae Ling sending them to a sinkhole.

"I think that may be a very smart decision," Toby agreed.

Melissa didn't want to be odd-woman-out, and she certainly didn't look forward to exploring this hole, any more than she'd wanted to see the madman's cellar, but they couldn't just drop this lead. "We would be going in, then, as his invited guests?"

"*You* would be going in as his invited guest," Toby answered. "He's not that excited about seeing me again. I had to bang one of his buddies on the head to get in the first time. Nor is he excited about meeting Christian. He seems to think his business is with you alone."

"No way do I let you go down alone!" Christian's tone didn't invite any argument.

"Do you think Inspector Dwighton will smoke him out any time soon?" Melissa definitely wanted a workable alternative.

"No cop, in his right mind, would go down there, alone or with a whole SWAT team." Toby wiped that bit of daydreaming off the agenda. "The place is parceled into separate little forts, which would have to go down one at a time. We're not talking ideal siege conditions, as anyone who's fought house-to-house in a war at midnight will tell you."

Melissa turned full-face to Toby in the back. "*You* went in and came out."

"And I'll give thanks on bended knees for a very long time to come!" Obviously, he didn't want her to get the impression he looked forward to repeating the miracle.

Melissa didn't like coming this far only to find she was kept from learning something by her lack of nerve. "What if we took it a step at a time and turned back if it got too hairy?"

"This woman is real?" It wasn't obvious if Toby thought her

very brave or very stupid.

"If Sylint has something to say, and he's willing to say it, I want to hear it." She sounded braver than she was. Nonetheless, this seemed less daunting than it might have if she'd not already survived so much. On the other hand, wasn't it dangerous to get jaded to danger?

"You have any reason to suspect him homicidal?" Christian didn't want her going in there, but he definitely didn't want her going in without him along for support.

"No habeas corpus if that's what you mean. Word is, he handles drugs better than most. However, it's my experience that any addict is completely different from one second to the next."

"I say we at least take a look." She couldn't believe she was ready to take the chance; but, there it was.

"Did you think to bring a gun, Melissa?" Toby's not unfriendly smile told her he read how his suggestion socked home reality. He showed her his Walther PP in its shoulder holster beneath his sweater.

"I don't own a gun." It was only after all that had happened that she seriously entertained getting one.

"I've one." Christian stretched to pop the glove compartment for his Colt automatic. He checked its clip to make sure it was loaded.

"Am I to take this as a go?" Toby sounded as if, one way or the other, it was their decision.

"Melissa?" Christian gave her a chance to change her mind.

"It's a go," she said.

There was a sudden rap on the window by one of the kids who'd sprawled atop Toby's car. Melissa's keyed-up condition could be measured by how high she jumped at the sound.

Toby rolled down the window. "Hey, kid, the lady here is thinking of going down the rat hole for a look-see. What do you think?"

The kid shrugged. "People go down and up all of the time, don't they?"

Toby's frown indicated he did not appreciate the kid's evaluation. "So, why are you banging on my window?" he demanded in a none-too-friendly tone.

"You've a phone in that junk heap of yours that thinks you're there to answer it."

"Right!" He opened the door, stepped out, and called behind him: "You two think it over."

"So, do we calmly go over pros and cons?" Christian wanted to know.

"Aren't you a little curious about what Sylint has to say that we may lose if we don't go in after it?"

"Yes, but I'm not overly enthused by the woman I love scrounging around potentially dangerous surroundings to hear him say it."

"I just hate to let the opportunity pass if it looks more dangerous than it is."

"You want a look, we'll take it, but I want you to listen to Toby and me if we decide it's not working out."

Toby climbed back into the car. "A green Volkswagen van, stolen two days ago from Samuel Tollins on Keith Road, was just located abandoned off Highway One. Its license matches the one you gave me and belongs to a Toyota pickup ripped off a gardener at Simon Fraser University three days ago. All indications are that you were dealing with people intent upon covering their tracks and knowing how to do it."

Melissa was glad there were no easy trails to Mae Ling. The woman's efforts deserved that much. They, also, deserved a complete follow-up.

"Flashlight!" Toby identified and held his, brought from his car. "Any on board this heap?"

Melissa had seen Christian go back to his car for one when Carol and she had been unable to distinguish John and him in

the darkness adjoining the service station. Since she'd not seen it
in the glove compartment with the gun, she asked Christian,
"Under the seat?"

He nodded and reached down to bring it out.

"Shall we get our house calls over for the day?" Toby
recognized that a decision had been made. He opened the door
and got out.

He gave instructions to the two kids as Christian and
Melissa joined him. "I come back and find these two cars in one
piece, you are going to be two very happy and much richer little
snakes. I come back and they're stripped down for parts, you're
grass and I'm the lawnmower. Got it?"

"You think this is a Clint Eastwood movie?" One kid wasn't
noticeably impressed.

"Yea, and I'm waiting for *you* to make *my* day!"

Toby crossed the street. He proceeded as if he'd voted with
the majority. *That,* Melissa decided, was pure pro.

She and Christian followed through the charred door and
into a murky interior where sunshine entered only as dust-filled
shafts through a collapsed, rotten roof and damaged, crumbly
walls.

"Another thing: this building is condemned, so don't be
surprised if parts of it should collapse on you, now and again."
He didn't look or act afraid, though, as he lead them to the
stairwell that now only led in one direction—down.

The beginning was not as bad as Melissa expected. It was
pretty straightforward down several flights of steps. There was
plenty of junk and debris, but constant up-and-down foot
traffic had cleared a recognizable trail.

After going through the door three levels down, things got
less obliging.

"Fun time!" Toby announced and stopped for everyone to
get adjusted to a darkness more wide open than that confined
within the stairwell.

He put cupped hand to his mouth and shouted. "Coming in Sylint! with a couple visitors. You at home and hospitable?"

"You do not have to shout, man," someone said so close beside Melissa that her jump of surprise almost separated her from her skin.

Toby and Christian were just as surprised if their swift swings of flashlights were any indication.

The spotlighted old man, arms uplifted, stood beside an old packing crate not four feet from Melissa.

She was relieved Sylint had met her halfway.

The old man, missing one front tooth and every hair on his head, disappointed with, "Sylint's awaiting and says you're to take her through."

"We don't want any trouble." Melissa thought that a necessary assurance.

"Then, don't let your friends go shooting their guns without a by-your-leave." It was obvious he saw very clearly in darkness Melissa would have found debilitating without the flashlights.

He was gone so suddenly that the lights couldn't follow. The empty beams swept this way and that but revealed nothing but the eerie glow of a cat's eyes; the cat screeched and hissed its unfriendly hello.

"Welcome!" Toby sounded as if he'd been there before and was not happy to be back. "If you'd be kind enough to step this way, please." He shined his light in the direction he wanted them to go.

For the first time, Melissa sensed the presence of more watchers than just a cat and the snaggletoothed old man. Her dismay relayed itself to Toby without any words being spoken.

"Oh, yes, they're there," he assured. "They wonder what we're up to and if they can somehow take advantage. For most, blown out of their minds, it'll be just the mind-trip. Others . . ."

"I think we've come far enough," she came to a stop. She was gutsy, but she was no fool, and she didn't want these two men hurt because she'd pulled them down there with her. "If Sylint has anything to say, let . . ."

Someone or something grabbed her ankles and gave a pull. She went down with a thud that banged her head and knocked her breath away.

"Melissa!" Christian and Toby shouted in unison.

Their lights tried to find her. The beams were segmental diagonals as Melissa's flaying hands and arms hit confining top, bottom, and sides of the narrow slideway through which she was dragged downward toward deeper and more oppressive darkness.

9

The slide became steeper, until pulling her ankles was no longer required to provide downward momentum. When she ejected, like a laundry bag from its chute, she had visions of a waiting cement floor. What she hit was a soft mattress that smelled sour and looked uninviting when illuminated by the light from the door immediately opened to one side of the room she was in.

"If you please, Miss Jordan?" someone invited from behind the light. "Galin, give her a hand!"

Galin was the snaggletoothed, bald old man. It didn't take Melissa long to figure he was the White Rabbit who'd jerked her down this rabbit hole.

Christian and Toby called her from a seemingly great distance.

"Please, don't call back," the voice behind the light warned.

"Mr. Sylint?" she attempted a delaying tactic.

"Please, don't tarry, either," he insisted. "I told your friend I had no intentions of making this a group session, so . . ."

Christian and Toby were obviously now in the chute; she heard their ongoing descent.

While she hesitated, eager for them to join her, Lenny Sylint showed his disapproval by slowly beginning to shut the door on her.

"No, wait!"

He paused just long enough to let her slip through behind Galin.

She tried to make out his features, but it was difficult while he and Galin barricaded the door. When he finally did turn, he looked forty-something but might have been younger; the lighting didn't flatter his complexion which probably was an unhealthy yellow in the best circumstances. His hair, might have been black or brown; it was definitely lank and to his shoulders. His bony frame looked as if it could stand more weight and probably had at one time.

Melissa was startled by a loud bang against the closed door.

"Melissa!" It was Christian.

"Tell your friends you'll join them shortly," Lenny told her.

She put her cheek against the door as another thump reverberated cool metal. "I'm okay, Christian! You and Toby are supposed to wait there."

"You hurt her, Sylint, and you answer to me!" Christian punctuated with another pound.

Lenny didn't look impressed. Why should he? He was walled behind a metal door not likely to be breached in a hurry. "If you'd step this way." He motioned her to precede him.

"Lenny?" Galin's supplication was an unbecoming whine; it was rewarded with a small packet of white substance which he put behind his back as if Lenny might change his mind.

Lenny's laugh was neither malicious nor mirthful. It was as if he had felt one appropriate for the occasion but had unsuccessfully tried to summon it up. He picked up a Coleman lantern, nodded Melissa ahead, and left Galin uncomplaining in the darkness at the door.

It took longer than Melissa expected, upstairs, downstairs, through cluttered halls and comparatively clean ones, past myriad open and closed doors that offered no hints of what lurked within. Each step, she wondered if she hadn't made a big mistake. She'd be hard-pressed to find her way back, even with light. However, there was no question but that she was now fully committed.

"How much farther?" she asked finally.

"No farther." He nodded toward the door a few feet away; it, like the other, was metal. It was fit with double locks. "Can't take too many precautions," Lenny explained. "Someone actually tried to ax me the other night. Guy with a *Nam Raider* tattoo and mighty full pockets. He still has his tattoo, plus a large bump on his head, but his pockets are noways nearly as full."

"The man who gunned down Elizabeth Howard had a *Nam Raider* tattoo."

"Coincidence?" His question was not-hardly-likely.

He motioned her inside and followed her in.

There were overstuffed chairs, a couch, an end table, a coffee table, several throw rugs; all looked a little ratty. More odds-and-end furniture materialized as he lit candles before calling the Coleman light, "Too harsh!" and turning it off.

Melissa wondered what he was on. He seemed coherent enough, except his complexion was sickly, his eyes too dilated even for the now non-glare lighting.

"Sit down." A wave of his hand suggested any of the alternatives; she chose the closest chair.

He wound an old Victrola. She was afraid he'd play one of those wailing chromatic-scale pieces Kevin had preferred. He surprised with Strauss.

"You remind me of a waltz person," he said and sat in the

chair across from her.

Rather than romanticize his features, the flickering candles made him appear more wizard-in-his-lair. The music seemed completely out of place.

"Kevin once said you were someone best imagined twirling, twirling in a white ball gown. He was quite the romantic, you know? Not even Nam took it all out of him. How beautiful his artwork was, to have been born among so much horror."

"Yes," she agreed.

"I'd offer you a little something, being so flush at the moment, but Kevin told me your attitude on drugs, so I'll save us both the embarrassment."

She swallowed the sarcasm he tempted. "Mae Ling seems to think you have something to tell me." Melissa wanted this over and done. She felt safe enough right now, but the atmosphere was oppressive. "From what Toby says, you think so, too."

He shut his eyes and rested his head against the back of his chair. "Kevin and I went to this bar in Chinatown; place called *Phant Tai*. Kevin would come out with me for a drink every so often, even if he were clean and I was flying high. He was never one to get uppity around those of us less able to kick the habit. He knew we all had our own ghosts to battle the best way we knew how. Besides, he was gloomy about you being comatose in the clinic."

The waltz ended. Lenny didn't bother to restart it, merely waiting for the machine to run down.

"Captain Steven E.T. Miller," he said the moment the record stopped. "A real bad penny if the mere sight of him, and his sight of Kevin, could put Kevin back on drugs."

"You do know Captain Miller has been officially declared dead in the helicopter crash I went down in?"

"I know that's what Kevin read. I, also, know what Kevin said he saw that evening in the *Phant Tai* that put him back on drugs after over a year of being clean."

"Did *you* see Captain Miller?" She figured it had to be drugs talking.

His eyes, now open, looked unfocused; she thought she was losing him.

"I left Kevin for only a few minutes," he said. "When I got back to the table, Kevin was close to panic. Said he'd seen a ghost. Said E.T. was back from the dead. I thought he meant the green critter in the movie, and I assured him E.T. was safely back in E.T.-land.

"He meant Captain E.T. Miller, though, who'd been in and out before I got back."

Melissa's goose bumps were large as gooseberries. "You're sure this took place *after* the helicopter went down?"

"That's all he'd read about in the papers: a U.S. helicopter, on loan to a super-secret Canadian laboratory, down with a meteorite, a prominent gallery owner, and one of Vancouver's wealthiest men: the stuff front-page headlines are made of. As I said, you were comatose."

"Kevin was positive it was Miller?" Impossible!

"So much so that he wanted something to calm his nerves. I tried to talk him out of it, but he was beyond listening to reason.

"It was after he shot up that he told me he was a goner for sure.

"Said the first time he met Captain E.T. Miller was when Kevin had just shipped into Nam. Miller was considered a must-to-meet in Saigon, because anyone who wanted a good time in that city, no matter what kind, supposedly fattened the captain's pocketbook. Evidently he had connections in very high places; Kevin said the captain would have needed every one of them if he were mixed up in only half the illegalities attributed to him. Kevin once commented to a Lance Corporal Brent that if the captain had so many connections, why was he still a captain. Brent said that captains didn't have nearly the spotlight on them as generals.

"Brent was at the same transit depot as Kevin. They were both waiting for permanent assignments, but Brent had been through the routine before. He'd received a leg wound at the front, been shipped to Saigon for patch-up, and he was about to go back in. He was not, to put it mildly, excited by the idea. He figured to buy his way out of combat, because the captain could get him assigned to a plush, behind-the-lines desk job for the rest of Brent's tour of duty—for the very low cost of only twenty-thousand U.S. dollars. Brent was raising the money by running dope for the captain to the guys at the hospital and at the transit depot.

"Brent was always worried he wasn't going to come up with all the money in time, and when his and Kevin's assignments came through early, he really panicked. He disappeared from the barracks one night, a couple of days before they were scheduled to ship out, and Kevin figured he'd gone AWOL. Except, he turned up the next day to say the captain, at that very minute, was fixing the paperwork. A few drinks, and he said he'd earned the last of his needed cash by doing the captain a little favor.

"Sure enough, according to Kevin, Brent didn't ship out with him to Chai Mai.

"When Kevin flew back into Saigon a couple of months later, for some badly needed rest and recuperation, most of the other guys in his unit had bit the dust, and he had no desire to follow suit.

"He tracked down Brent who, by then, was no walking advertisement for the plush life behind lines. He could barely remember who Kevin was. When Kevin let it be known he was willing to do the captain whatever 'little' favors necessary to get reassigned out of the battle zone, Brent told Kevin he was better off fighting Cong in the jungle than doing favors for the captain in Saigon.

"Then, he told Kevin that the captain killed Vietnamese

women, commanded by little voices in his head beamed to him direct 'from extraterrestrials in outer space.' Kevin didn't believe it. Brent asked him just why he thought the captain ran around with a moniker like E.T. It was because of the extraterrestrial voices he had buzzing around in his head; voices he said that saved his life in Cambodia and, again, when he got caught in friendly fire; voices that told him how to set up his vice network. If those voices, in turn, demanded a bit of easily arranged payment fo their services, now and again, the captain wasn't going to think twice about shorting Vietnam a few of its women.

"Kevin still figured Brent was trying to scare or test him. Even if what he told Kevin were true, Kevin said he'd seen enough dying at the line to accept a bit more of it behind the lines, if that's what it took to get him through the next few months alive. Brent shrugged and told him to meet him later, and they'd talk more."

The chills had begun a cascade through Melissa and wouldn't stop.

"But Brent didn't show, so Kevin approached the captain, himself. The captain told him that before he'd do anything to help Kevin, he had to prove his loyalty by doing a little job for him. Kevin agreed. But when the captain gave him a chilling assignment, Kevin knew Brent had been right. It wasn't worth it. When he told the captain, he couldn't to the job, the captain said it was too late. Do it or else. Scared Kevin carried it out. Later, Brent turned up dead, riddled with knife wounds. Anxious to get out of Saigon, Kevin shipped back to Chai Mai and was in a POW camp within a cuople weeks' time.

"The next Kevin heard of the captain was that he'd gone down piloting the helicopter on which you and Wynard were aboard. It was *the* captain, all right. Granted, there were no pictures, but Kevin said guys like him were always leery about having their pictures taken; besides, photos of the

Vancouverites involved—you and Wynard—made better press.
But, there was the synopsis of his service record: all those years
in Nam when no one, without ulterior motives, would have ever
re-upped for all that run-on duty in a house of horrors; still a
captain after all his supposedly honorable service in a war where
lowly corporals could be elevated to acting-captains overnight.

"Then, who does Kevin spot in a bar in Vancouver's
Chinatown merely hours after he's officially declared dead? The
captain!"

Melissa recalled Captain Miller and knew, without doubt,
that the madman with the cold eyes, who had kidnapped her
and Carol, then left them to kill Kevin, had *not* been the same
man who'd piloted the helicopter. *Kevin had to have been
wrong!* "The police found drugs." Mind-distorting drugs *had* to
be the difference.

"They were the *wrong* drugs, weren't they?" he argued.

The room, with its flickering lights, made Lenny, with his
knowing smile, look macabre.

"I know the universal misconception that an addict is an
addict is an addict, but we have our personal preferences, and if
Kevin had had the bread, he wouldn't have dealt coke, because
heroin was what got his motor running. My guess: the captain
planted the coke. Did I tell you, my man with the *Nam Raider*
tattoo had several packets of high-quality coke in his pockets
with all that cash? What do you suppose he'd have done with it
if I'd not been a black belt in karate?"

"You don't think the police might find any or all of this of
interest?"

"Kevin was an addict. I'm an addict. This is a tale of
resurrection as witnessed by that addict, as told to this addict,
who is telling it to you. Will the police believe? You tell me!"

Melissa knew the answer. "Story-time's over. The captain is
a real snake and I have no intentions of letting him kill me for
what I know."

Galin appeared on cue, his eyes dilated to the size of saucers. Melissa preferred Lenny of the two, but he was obviously through with her, having performed whatever service he felt he owed Kevin's memory.

Galin wanted her hand, and she was more than a little loathe to turn it over. "Get lost in here, missy, and the chances aren't so good you'll ever see topside," he said.

So, she surrendered, and the tightness of his grip indicated he wasn't ever going to let loose.

He returned her to the world she couldn't see. She tripped more than once in the darkness, once on something alive enough to groan its protest. She couldn't imagine Galin knowing where he was, let along where he was going. Nonetheless, there was no hesitation on his part as he pulled her along.

"Wait here!" His handhold, that had seemed forever, was suddenly gone; she seemed completely adrift without it.

Her equilibrium deserted her, and she sat down, rather than fall down. She listened, expecting at least rats, but hearing nothing, until . . .

"If she's not where you say she is, I'll come through this place with a Roto-Rooter!"

"Christian!" She struggled to her feet.

"Melissa?"

She saw his flashlight. "Over here!" Its cool beam was like sunshine. His arms around her were like down-filled safety nets. His kiss was the final flame to liberate the iciness in her bones.

"Are you all right?" He breathed against her ear.

"Fine." She held him closer, her anchor in the storm. "Now."

Toby was less certain of his well-being. "Here's someone not fine until he's out of here. So, where is our guide to get us through this hole?"

"Right here!" Galin informed them and posed within the

flashlight beams that immediately found him. "Your out is that way!" He pointed through the doorway in which he stood. Then, like part of a magician's act, he disappeared.

Melissa remembered what happened the last time he'd disappeared, and she had no desire to stick around to see what he'd come up with for encores.

Christian echoed his companion's sentiments: "Let's move on out of here!"

Through the door was a stairwell leading up and down. As there wasn't a temptation available to coax them down, they headed up as fast as their legs could run the gauntlet of garbage.

That their way out wasn't their way in became evident when the stairs deteriorated to rubble toward the end. They reached the outside in a hands-and-knees scramble that deposited them far back in the building.

Inspector Dwighton waited at their cars. So, too, did the two kids who looked as if the inspector would rip off both autos if they turned their attention off him for a minute.

"No need, I suppose, to ask where you chimney sweeps have been plying your trade, or if you have permits for the firearms you're so obviously carrying."

"We took a vote and decided we had a better chance of interviewing Sylint than you did." Melissa's clothes, arms, legs, and probably her face, were streaked with soot, and, she'd thought Lenny and Galin looked like something the cat dragged in.

"You're probably right in your assessment," the inspector agreed. "I am, however, amazed by your willingness to go where angels, and certainly this policeman, would fear to tread."

She told him everything Lenny had said; Christian and Toby listened while the latter peeled off several large-denomination bills and handed them to the kids who looked satisfied their vigil had been worth it.

What she expected the inspector to say was pretty much what Lenny had expected him to say. But he surprised her. "What do you make of this tale of the resurrected helicopter pilot?"

"I met the man while he was flying us and supplies. He didn't have the eyes of the guy who kidnapped Carol and me, and the way I figure, it was our kidnapper who left us to take out Kevin. So, either Kevin was mistaken, or I am."

"Maybe your kidnapper sent someone to kill Kevin, like he sent someone to blow you away when the bullets mistakenly took out Elizabeth," Christian suggested.

"The use of the meteorite knife on Kevin, as opposed to a machine gun, tells me that there was no such substitution."

"You think your helicopter pilot could have lived such a sordid life in Nam, Melissa?" Christian asked.

"I've only his eyes to go on. If they weren't those of our kidnapper, that's not to say they excused him of a sordid past."

"Next time, think twice about playing Alice down the rabbit hole," Inspector Dwighton warned. "For all your effort, you could have come up with a more realistic story than Lenny Sylint and his addiction whispered in your ear."

"So you have any new breakthroughs to share with us?" Christian asked the inspector. "Turnabout, as they say, is fair play."

"Not when I'm the policeman and you're the recalcitrant civilians without a need to know." Apparently, he had second thoughts. "Although, there's no harm in telling you Kevin's girl friend has seemingly dropped off the edge of the earth. We suspect her uncle had something to do with it. Evidently, he's Gop Ling, a man we've been trying to implicate in multiple car thefts, and he has a knack for hiding things."

He headed back to his car which, somehow, during its short stop, had come up missing two of its hub caps. His opinion of the area, in general, and its low-life residents, in particular, turned the air blue as Christian and Melissa headed to the penthouse. Toby drove off with warnings that Christian better check bank vaults to make sure there were funds to cover his fee.

"Can I borrow your phone?" She asked the operator to dial CanTech.

"Think it's time to check in with the colonel for running interference with the tattooed machine-gunner?"

"Among other things." She was distracted by the almost mechanical CanTech voice that asked if it could be of assistance.

Her request for Colonel Sampson in medical brought a one-minute, please, followed by a good three minutes of silence.

"Think they've lost him like they lost their meteorite?" Christian teased.

"Don't forget you weren't too successful in holding on to yours," Melissa reminded. She was going to tell him he had a grease smear down the right side of his face, but there was nothing he could do about it until he had soap and hot water, so she didn't bother.

"Are you being helped?" It wasn't the colonel, but she decided to pretend, anyway. "Colonel Sampson, it's Melissa Jordan."

"One moment, please." Melissa settled in for the duration that proved surprisingly short-lived.

"Miss Jordan?" Not that she'd yet lucked out with whom she wanted.

"I was hoping I might make arrangements to see Colonel Sampson some time tomorrow. He was transferred there from the Feaswell Clinic, I believe."

"How does tomorrow at eleven-hundred sound?"

It sounded as if Melissa had *finally* lucked onto someone in authority. "That'd be great."

"We'll have a pass in your name at the entrance gate and

someone the front desk to take you in."

She was surprised how easy.

Christian had the gist of the conversation. "Be careful at CanTech. I hear, it's harder to get out of there than out of a mere rat hole."

John had just left the penthouse when they arrived. Carol was headed back inside but spotted them and waited. She looked them up and down. "Dare I ask what happened?"

"Melissa will supply the grimy details." Christian wiped his face and only enlarged the sooty damage. "In the meantime, I'll go in search of a tub of my own, and some clean clothes, before taking you both out to supper."

"I'm afraid it's something ordered in for me tonight and an early-to-bed." Carol did look beat. "But don't let me stop you."

"Something in and early-to-bed *does* sound inviting," Melissa said. After what they'd been through today she didn't think Christian could possibly feel slighted.

She was right. "It has been an over-productive day, hasn't it? So, why don't we wait until tomorrow? I'll call you to coordinate our time."

His kiss and hug left some of his soot on Melissa's cheek while claiming some of hers for his. He saw them into the elevator before he headed back to his car.

Melissa filled in Carol, and vice versa, during the bath-to-supper routine that led to bedtime. Carol had brought over a couple suitcases of clothes, from which she offered Melissa her pick; an offer which, considering Melissa's present state of deteriorated wardrobe, was eagerly accepted. Carol, also, had money; some of which she loaned Melissa.

"My parents will be in the day after tomorrow." Carol drank the last of the hot chocolate left from her meal. "It'll be a simple memorial service, just family and a few friends. Of course, Mae Ling won't be able to attend, because she's . . ."

"It's all going to come together, you'll see." That promise, which she really didn't see much chance of happening anytime soon, was accompanied by a reassuring hug. "Right now, you just get a good-night's rest."

"Did I mention that John wants me to let him do plastic surgery?" Melissa's look said she hadn't. She flattened her hand across the knife cuts concealed by her buttoned negligee. "He says he can assure no evidence of scarring, and do it at cost. Actually . . ." She blushed just a trifle. ". . . he wanted to do it free, but . . ."

"I know what you mean about freebies." Melissa still had her clinic bill she suspected would never get to her unless she made some additional effort. Then again, the average person at Feaswell Clinic should have been so lucky?

"Well, it's really bed for me." Carol placed the now-empty cup on the table.

Melissa waited until Carol was almost to the bedroom. "Kind of like him, do you? John, I mean."

Carol smiled. "Kind of like him, do you? Christian, I mean."

Melissa gave her a wide grin in confirmation.

Melissa went upstairs to bed but couldn't sleep. She ended up at a Rococo-style secretaire which was probably as antique and expensive as it looked. She used several sheets of thick and creamy bond paper from one of the parquetry drawers on which to sketch the scrimshaw design ideas that somehow congealed in her mind overburdened with so many other things.

Those completed, she tried sleep again, this time with such success that once again Carol was up and gone before Melissa greeted the new day.

She would have died for a tub bath, but she was running late. She settled for a shower and a change into Carol's clothes she'd picked out the night before. Actually, she turned out pretty good in the curdled-cream sheath with black borders at neck, armholes, and hem but the rattan-weave sandals pinched more than a bit but she tried not to notice.

A cab had her at the CanTech front gate for her visitor's pass by quarter of eleven. She was at the front desk by ten-of. At five-of, she was joined in reception by, "I'm Jerry McLean." He had a tan seldom seen outside a tropical paradise which was accentuated by the vibrant orange of his CanTech uniform.

"Acapulco," he responded to her combination query/compliment and ushered her into one of the bank of elevators. "I can only stand so much of Vancouver's gloom and doom before I have to flee to sunshine."

He knew where she was going, but if he were the least curious as to why, he didn't show it. If he recognized her from her photos that had graced every local paper and had flashed across every TV's morning, noon, and late-night news, he didn't show that, either. Maybe he'd been in Acapulco during her trauma-time.

"Melissa!" Colonel Sampson looked no less military in a hospital gown, in a hospital room far more Spartan than any at the Feaswell Clinic. He had a bandage on his neck and a sling on his left arm. All other visible damage was concealed by the sheet pulled to his chest. "How nice of you to stop by! Truth is, I was going to call you for a little chat, so I'm extra pleased you beat me to the punch."

She sat in the chair Jerry pulled up before leaving. "I couldn't let too many days pass without letting you know how I appreciate your fast action at the clinic. There's no doubt you're the reason I'm alive today."

"I should have been faster," he judged with a too-bad shake of his head. "Poor Elizabeth . . . Truth is, I'd grown stale, behind a desk too long."

"If that's the case, I pity anyone who comes up against you when you're battle-ready."

"Thank-you very much." His tone was modest.

Melissa couldn't help suspecting a good deal of skillful

playacting went into the makeup of this man. Would she want to know the probably tough-as-nails real man beneath? She thought not.

"Now about this little talk of ours." His smile could probably have charmed a less suspicious listener. "I have a bit of good news I'd like you to pass on to Mr. Wynard, if you would. Namely, it seems I was grossly misinformed about the cause of Captain Miller's death."

He certainly had her interest with that one.

"Not the chap's fault who performed the initial autopsy, you understand." His was the buck-stops-here tone of voice. "Unless one is *really* proficient in bomb cases, this could easily have been mistaken for one, which it was. Yesterday, however, we had a couple experts flown in who insist all the damage could have resulted from simple impact. So, our apologies for jumping to conclusions that proved unwarranted and flawed after all the facts were in."

"Shouldn't you be telling this to Christian?" It wasn't Melissa who'd been accused of booby-trapping the helicopter.

"Officially, charges were never made, don't you see? Therefore, officially, apologies can't be rendered. Follow?"

Melissa wasn't pleased she'd been responsible for worrying Christian over nothing, no matter how glad she was to hear the Colonel recant.

"It's all unfortunate." He looked her directly in the eyes, but she suspected a military course, Eye Contact 202, made such I'm-sincere techniques possible with a whole lot of practice. "Of course, if you failed to relay to Mr. Wynard the misinformation . . ." He could obviously tell by her expression he shouldn't count on that. "Ah, so you do see how it's important someone put Mr. Wynard's mind to rest, and, hopefully, all's well that ends well.

"Speaking of which, we've decided, under these new circumstances, and under those I cited you earlier, not to pursue our initial suspicions that Wynard absconded with the meteorite tracked down by Elizabeth and you. Of course, I would personally be more satisfied if you could assure me the Nova Scotia meteorite was just that." He paused, apparently so she could render such assurances.

"Unfortunately, it was stolen before I could make the requested verification, but that he was so willing to show it to me convinces me you were barking up the wrong tree with that one, too."

"Well if my superiors are happy, I'm happy."

"I don't suppose it would be possible for me to see Captain Miller's body."

For once, his expression didn't look preplanned. "You?"

"Would that be possible?"

"Whatever for?" He tried to get his well-practiced facade back in place but didn't succeed quite yet.

"The police have heard the rumor that the captain was spotted in Vancouver after the helicopter went down."

"Impossible?"

"I thought, since I'd seen the captain around our camp site and could identify his body, I could set those rumors to rest."

"Hardly a pretty sight; an autopsied cadaver."

"I only need to see his face," she said, as if her having viewed Kevin's corpse had prepared her for all others.

He picked up the telephone and dialed two digits with that same hand. "This is Colonel Sampson. Could you give me the present disposition on Captain Steven Miller?"

Melissa couldn't believe it was this easy.

"Yes, I'll wait."

The body, once seen, would assure Melissa of two things: Kevin hadn't been killed by Captain Miller; Carol and she hadn't been kidnapped by him, either; although, she was already sure of both.

"I see," the colonel said finally. "Under whose order? And

was the family notified? I see."

He hung up, and Melissa knew there'd be no definitive answers after all.

"He was cremated this morning." If his perplexed expression were fake, it was excellent fake.

"Under whose order?" Melissa wasn't sure it mattered, but she figured to follow through for whatever information she could get from him.

"General Kenteth."

"Was the family notified?"

"Seems Captain Miller was a foundling with no listed next-of-kin."

"I'm sorry." Sorry he was a foundling; sorry he was dead; sorry he was cremated before she was able to clear him with proof-positive.

"I'm sure there's been a mistake if anyone says they saw him alive after the accident," the colonel assured her.

No need to tell him the source was hearsay, possibly drug-induced. If the colonel wanted to know badly enough, he'd make the necessary few calls required to find the answers for himself.

She stood to leave. "Yes, I suppose so."

"Would you like me to call Jerry to show you the way out?"

Anyone who had managed the maze of a burned-down-building basement could figure her way out of here. "I take a right out the door, a left at the second hall branching; it's the first elevator on the right, down to the main floor."

If she expected rules and regulations that required all non-personnel to be escorted, at all times, she was mistaken. "Right!" was all he said.

She put the chair back where Jerry had found it. "And thanks again, Colonel Sampson."

"My pleasure." Said with all apparent sincerity and accompanied by a snappy salute.

At the elevator, Melissa was joined by a tall, slim woman whose neatly cropped red hair somehow managed not to clash with the orange of her CanTech uniform. She smiled and hugged a file folder as if someone might, at any moment, make an attempt to swipe it.

"Corporal!" someone called as the elevator arrived.

Melissa and the redhead turned in unison.

"Yes, sir," the woman replied as the man joined her.

"Just a spot-check for authorization, corporal." He turned toward Melissa. "You're free to proceed, ma'am."

"I could hold the elevator," she volunteered.

"Not necessary, ma'am. The corporal will take the next one."

Melissa stepped in and pushed MF.

The doors slid shut, and the elevator dropped so suddenly that Melissa didn't need warning bells to tell her something was wrong; her stomach lodged in her throat in déjà-vu reminiscence of that other horror ride when helicopter, so much dead weight, had dropped her out of the sky.

In staccato, consecutive blinks, emphasized by the increasing velocity, numbered lights hypnotized with their foreboding of disaster, 4, 3, 2, 1 . . . and the ground rushed prematurely up to meet her.

10

There was nothing like on-site experimentation to prove there was no chance of saving yourself in a runaway elevator by jumping up at moment of impact. Something about the mad ride down wasn't conducive to jumping, let alone coordinating any such response with meeting the bottom of the shaft.

Melissa expected to die when she saw the basement "B" light flash on bright as day. She was encouraged to see the subbasement "SB1" which had hardly been discernable before its light came on. Discovering an SB2, as well, would have encouraged more if it had been accompanied by the elevator showing any indications of slowing down.

When the loud grunts and groans of mechanical system in malfunction was joined by frantic vibrations of walls, ceiling, and floor all around her, Melissa was sure her moment of truth was at hand.

A series of jerky partial stops confused her remaining sense of balance, and she ended up on the floor.

Finally, the elevator stopped altogether amid more noises than Melissa cared to analyze.

She imagined herself caught somewhere between floors, and she couldn't have been more amazed when the doors slid open to reveal SB4 and a man who, white-haired and orange-suited, proved less surprised to see her than she was to see him.

"Melissa Jordan?"

She would have never guessed, by his attitude, that she was down and almost out on the floor, looking like a rag doll tossed to one side by a little girl no longer interested.

"I don't believe we've been formally introduced, have we?" She tried for levity, but it had come out unadulterated sarcasm.

She tried to scramble to her feet but discovered her momentarily-converted-to-rubber legs weren't up to the chore; she went down again.

If she thought he might be gentlemanly enough to help her, she was wrong.

"I'm afraid we don't have much time." He produced some pieces of folded paper and handed them down.

"Let me guess," she said. "You want my autograph."

He didn't crack a smile. He looked very nervous. "Tell Christian I'm sorry about this, but it's the only way I could think to get it out."

"This?" She might have unfolded the paper she waved up at him, but she was conserving energy for her next attempt to get up.

"A copy of Miller's medical report," he informed. "No way I can get it out. You though . . ." He looked over his shoulder as if he expected someone at any moment. He stepped to the control board and pulled open a hinged panel that revealed a red telephone. "Tell them the elevator malfunctioned and lodged at SB4. They'll send someone. Do it now, so they won't suspect you of wandering somewhere you shouldn't. It wouldn't do to have them give you a strip search and find that."

Melissa now doubted the redhead had been detained by mere accident.

He reached for the telephone and handed the receiver down to her.

"I'm stuck!" she informed a mechanical voice that quickly became less so. She was kept talking, undoubtedly to make sure she stayed put, all the while assured help was on the way.

Her scrambled condition was obvious when she spent more time marveling as to how weird her mail deliveries, since the postal strike, than in hiding the paper handed over by the now-disappeared-faster-than-Galin delivery man. She hardly had the paperwork tucked into her pantyhose waistband than two security men appeared to give her an assist.

With one's help, she regained her feet while the other took charge of the phone to report in.

They didn't take her to the main floor but to a security office on SB1 where she was offered apologies, a chair, a drink, and an aspirin; in that order. She refused all three and, then, refused the doctor suggested by Sergeant Wenelson who sounded much younger on the telephone than the salt-and-pepper-haired, slightly paunchy reality.

She went over the occurrences leading up to where she was, conveniently omitting any mention of the man and what he'd given her.

The sergeant related an interesting bit of trivia about miners in South Africa who made it a contractual point never to trust elevators to computers; they demanded human hands-on.

"They're to be commended on their foresight." She'd recovered enough to be anxious to be gone. Somehow, inside CanTech, with CanTech paperwork that CanTech might, for whatever the reason, not want her to have, over-shadowed the residual horror of her express ride.

She suspected the sergeant would have held her longer if she'd driven there on her own. As she'd come by cab, he seemed satisfied her condition wouldn't contribute to any traffic accidents on the way home for which CanTech might, for whatever the reason, be held liable. He was downright, appreciative when she told him she'd be happy to sign a release relieving CanTech, forever and ever, of legal responsibility. Little did he know that the last thing she wanted was litigation to bring out why the elevator had been programmed to malfunction in the first place.

There was no denying her audible sigh of relief when she was handed into the taxi, its door closed behind her, that drove her out the front gate as slick as a greased pig through the slats of its sty.

The supreme irony would have been getting caught with a CanTech document that Colonel Sampson had already made superfluous by his summation.

She leaned back, shut her eyes, and wondered what possibly could befall her during her cab ride. Considering her track record, she was thoroughly surprised when the trip proved uneventful. Nor did anyone wait to knock her on her head, push her into oncoming traffic, or shoot at her when she got out.

To further reassure that her day, ill-begun, showed definite signs of improvement was Christian's call, "Melissa!" as she unlocked the glass door to the small lobby. "Come on!" he said before she could get out her news.

He took her hand and had her down the walk before she got out, "Come on, where?"

"Seattle!"

That brought her up short? He had to be kidding, and she told him so.

"Really!" he insisted. "The company plane is fueled and waiting at the airport."

Even accepting spur-of-the-moment excitement, "Didn't it occur to you that I might need the ladies' room first?"

"Ooops!" He stopped and looked downright apologetic.

She laughed; she couldn't help herself. "As it happens, I might be able to wait until the airport."

"Good!" His hand still held hers, and they were off again toward his car down the street.

"Do you tell me why Seattle, why now, or do I tell you about my exciting morning and the bit of good news gleaned from it?"

"You go first."

"Where I should go, first, is to my condo for a change of clothes." She wasn't ready to move back in, but some basics were needed for even off-the-top-of-the-head trips to Seattle. "I should, also, stop at a bank."

"I've money enough for both of us." He opened the car door. "And I had my secretary stop by your condo to throw a few of your things into an overnight bag. She's meeting us at the plane."

"Well, you certainly think of everything," she said. She wasn't fond of a strange woman rifling her things, but, considering the police had been there before, what the heck!

"So, how exciting could it have been at CanTech?" He steered the car southeast along Beach. "Colonel Sampson chase you around his hospital bed?"

"No, but a friend of yours somehow rigged an elevator I was in so that I dropped from fifth floor to fourth sub-basement in fifteen-seconds flat."

"*My* friend?" He looked surprised and sounded concerned.

"That's the impression he gave when he didn't bother to pick me up off the floor but merely handed me a copy of Captain Miller's medical record."

"And *he* told *me* he couldn't possibly get hold of it, let alone smuggle it out!" It was obviously a compliment.

"He could have saved you, me, and him a lot of time and bother. Colonel Sampson had just finished telling me a more thorough examination of Miller's body revealed he was *not* a bomb victim as originally diagnosed." She finished off with more specifics.

After which, Christian confessed, "That does leave me breathing a little more easily."

He looked as if he expected her to produce the report; considering where it was stashed, a dress-lifting required to get at it, and considering its data was redundant, she told him he'd have to wait.

There was no easy way to the airport in a city that refused freeways inside its city limits. The route was a clutter of one-way streets, more often than not crowded with irate drivers. Usually it took longer to access the airport than to make whatever the flight at the other end.

Melissa, however, had no complaints. She was with the man she loved, and she had guarantees there would be no witch-hunt to connect him to something she'd known from the beginning he couldn't have done. Seattle, if not the most exotic destination in the world, offered a change of pace sufficient to have her looking forward to seeing it. She had a gallery there, but whether or not she checked in would depend on just what Christian had in mind. "Did you ever tell me why you decided to whisk me off to romantic Seattle?"

He stretched for the glove compartment and retrieved a back issue of *Time* and one of *Blade.* "There's an obituary in *Time,* page sixty."

"There happens to be several," she informed him when the pages were turned.

"The one on Charles Tefson, IV."

"Ah, yes. 'Prominent Seattle restauranteer died last Friday . . .' We're off to offer condolences?"

"Never met the man, although I've eaten at his restaurants, a time or two. I remember his veal Parmesan made me ill."

"Does that mean I cross off all fantasies of a romantic supper by candlelight?"

"Only as far as it will occur at any of the late Charles

Tefson's eateries."

"This *Blade* has some supplementary relevance?"

"Page seventeen."

"An article: *Prominent Bowie Knives from the Eighteen Hundreds.*"

"Paragraph fourteen, line three."

"Are you Sherlock Holmes to my Dr. Watson?" Nevertheless, nothing better to do in the squash of slow-moving traffic, she conducted the required search.

"See it?"

"You mean how it seems Mr. Tefson owned a Bill 'Bearhound' Canner bowie knife," Melissa confirmed. She read aloud: ". . . unique in that its blade was crafted from metal melted from a . . ."

" '. . . meteorite down in the Sierra Madre del Sur in 1896,' " they completed in unison.

"And guess what Lot #1246 is of the Tefson possessions to be auctioned off this very afternoon at the old homestead?" Christian asked.

She didn't need genius I.Q. for that one. "The Bearhound Bowie."

"Which means my meteorite stolen isn't necessarily the setback it need be."

"A knife in an auction is worth two in the stolen meteorite?" she paraphrased. "A meteorite knife is a meteorite knife is a meteorite knife to dangle in front of a madman with a fetish for meteorite knives?"

"I'm sure I can get my acquisition of it some kind of write-up in the press to let my father's killer . . ."

"And Kevin's killer," she reminded, "and the killer of who knows how many women, not to mention the man responsible for Elizabeth's death."

"I like the coincidence of this knife up for sale right now."

Melissa wasn't at all fond of "coincidence." Ever since her

kidnapper had seemed to savor it so, she'd been less than anticipatory as to what it might inadvertently drop in her lap; this knife no exception. Suddenly, she wasn't so keen on Seattle. Maybe if she asked really nice he'd head his company plane for Hawaii, she'd like a tan. "Maybe the killer relishes the coincidence, too."

"The only reason I came across this was because I've a staff paid to ferret out just such obscure meteorite-related tidbits."

"You think the killer doesn't have his own sources?"

"You do see, then, how this could be dangerous?"

"Yes, I see." Given that excuse to back out, she wasn't nearly as anxious for Hawaii.

"I figured you did. I, also, figured I didn't want to face the consequences of heading off to Seattle without you."

"Very smart man! If he's there, I want to be there to point the finger. His eyes are a dead give-away, take it from me."

"I've arranged for some professionals to be close at hand, just in case."

"So much for running off to Seattle with a man of my dreams for a romantic interlude." She sighed for dramatic effect.

"Well, two out of three ain't bad. Besides, if I were the guy I'd send someone to do my bidding for me. If that's the case, tracking him down will require a bit more subtlety, and we can retire to the candlelight for supper, after all."

He maneuvered through traffic which had grown thicker nearer the airport.

"There's still time for you to get a taxi and head back to the penthouse," he tried again. "I'd not only understand but be decidedly relieved in the bargain."

"We're in this together." She gave him a wide smile as thrilling adrenaline rushed inside her.

She was delighted to find his secretary, who awaited in a private lounge at the airport, wasn't the blonde-bombshell type.

Mrs. Carson, Melissa was definitely pleased by the Mrs., wasn't unattractive, but there was a no-nonsense, business attitude about her that Melissa immediately liked and found reassuring.

Christian saw Melissa's expression and made her smile even wider with, "Happily married for six years, with two beautiful children."

The small bag Mrs. Carson turned over had everything Melissa needed. If the secretary had any complaints about having to fetch it from a condo in which a murder had taken place so recently, she kept them to herself.

The company plane was a 707 with luxurious fittings. As the crow and a 707 flies it was only a little over a hundred miles to Seattle, so once the plane was airborne Melissa didn't waste time before she headed for the washroom. She changed into the gray, light wool suit Mrs. Carson apparently thought suited an auction, and she'd also supplied a plain white blouse, long-tailed ribbon bow tie, and black onyx cuff links. After putting up with aching feet, Melissa was relieved to find low-heeled black shoes.

On her way out, she gave Christian, on his way in, the pilfered medical report retrieved from safe-keeping in her pantyhose.

She was surprised when he reappeared so quickly.

"Tell me again," he said without looking up, "just what Colonel Sampson said about the cause of Miller's death."

She told him and could tell, even before he said more, that what the colonel said and what the document said were not one and the same.

"It states here, in no uncertain terms, that there is no doubt *whatsoever* that Miller was killed by one of at least two bombs planted on board the helicopter, one effectively antipersonnel."

"Effectively antipersonnel?"

He looked up. "Planted specifically to take out the pilot and having done so."

"But according to Colonel Sampson . . ." She stopped, figuring she had an explanation. "Your friend got you the old report."

Logical as that seemed, she wasn't encouraged by the shake of his head.

"You said two experts came in yesterday, right?"

"Right."

"Well, here's their opinions, and they confirm the initial investigative diagnosis."

He handed her the papers. Either it was wrong, and the dates were further indication *that* was unlikely, or the colonel had lied, but to what purpose? "Do you think he told me all of that to put you off-guard, the report faked to incriminate you?"

"I wish I knew what all those little CanTech people were up to?"

"He was so convincing. Although, I've thought from the beginning he could have made a great actor if the military hadn't taken him."

"I have Toby looking into the military aspects. I just won't call him off as quickly as I would have if I hadn't lucked onto this. Thanks, by the way!"

During landing, Melissa mulled the possibilities of a mad bomber joining the lineup of mad kidnapper and mad serial killer. She couldn't make him fit. When the chopper had gone down, there had been no one who wanted her dead; Kevin hadn't yet spilled any so-called secrets. Someone out to kill Christian couldn't have known beforehand he'd be on the chopper, because *Christian* hadn't known until fifteen minutes prior to takeoff; his team's search chopper had been sent back to Vancouver because of the bad weather, and the CanTech chopper had just lucked out with an unexpected break in the overcast.

"Maybe the bombs were supposed to kill Miller all along," Melissa said in a moment of revelation. "If even a little of what

Kevin said about him in Nam is true, he must have had plenty of enemies."

"You might just have hit the proverbial nail on the head!" Christian said.

There was a limo waiting when they cleared U.S. customs. For all the room available in it, Melissa and Christian took up surprisingly little. She sat next to him, her head on his shoulder; his hand was in her hair.

The geographical proximity of Seattle to Vancouver was manifest in the same overcast skies that usually dominated farther north. The milky light was additionally filtered by the limousine's tinted windows. Melissa definitely would have preferred Hawaii. Why couldn't Charles Tefson's obit have read: noted *Honolulu* restauranteer?

There was actually a patch of blue sky, and an attending wash of sunshine across a stretch of wide lawn, at Volunteer Park where the limo stopped before proceeding to the Tefson mansion. Melissa stood in the warmth but found it a poor substitute for the warmth of Christian's arms. Christian stood in conference with one of the four men hired to provide back-up. Two of the other men were already in place at the auction which had begun over two hours before. The fourth man was in the car parked in front of the limo at the curb; via walkie-talkie he received a running progress report on how near Lot #1246 was to the auction block.

"Did you notice anyone pay particular attention to the knife?" Christian wanted to know.

"Tefson had eclectic taste and it was displayed between a ten-carat, Colombia emerald ring and a miniature Russian icon. It was kind of hard to say who was interested specifically, as opposed to who was looking on the way by."

"Lot #1234!" the man called from the car.

"Right." Christian took Melissa's arm and walked her to the limo.

She slid in; he followed. The cars pulled simultaneously from the curb but went in opposite directions at the first crossroad, in order to stagger arrivals.

"There's still time to let me drop you off here," Christian reminded her. As possible danger loomed nearer, he thought her absence more and more preferable.

"Not a chance!" she said firmly. He'd been one-hundred percent correct when he'd thought she would have been unforgiving if he hadn't invited her along. She wanted whoever this killer/kidnapper/madman was in jail for a very, very long time! She wanted to help put him there, too.

They needed invitation to get them through the gates, and Christian produced one. The driver followed a circular roadway to deposit them at the front porch before he proceeded to the parking area.

The house was southern colonial with high ceilings, plaster walls, and large, spacious rooms. As public viewing of its contents had occurred over the preceding two days, most of the rooms were now roped off. Buyers and potential buyers were gathered in the downstairs ballroom where parquetry floors were padded to protect intricate woodwork from the scraping of metal folding chairs.

The items of immediate interest were lined up to the right of the auctioneer who concentrated on Lot #1237, a pair of Mayan vessels, with water fowl ornamental lids, from the northern Peten region, late Classic, circa A.D. 550-950.

Christian and Melissa stood near the back and gave the gathering a once-over; it was difficult for Melissa to pinpoint eyes in a landscape consisting mainly of well-coiffed heads.

She got a better viewpoint as an attendant led them down one of the aisles to their seats. Though some of the eyes not involved in the present bidding shifted in her direction, none possessed that cold, reptilian menace Melissa was sure she'd recognize.

The pre-Colombian bowls went for a price comparable to Melissa's quarterly income. The pottery was methodically shifted to the left where final paperwork was completed for the sale while Lot #1238 was brought centerstage. Inconspicuously, a member of the auctioneering coterie added another piece to the far right to keep the assembly line working.

Melissa wasn't positioned to see if the item of interest to Christian and her had yet entered the room.

"English silver," said the auctioneer, a distinguished man in well-tailored gray suit with plain, pale-blue tie. "Charles II cup and cover. Circa 1670. Height: eight-and-one-half inches. Shall we begin at four-thousand-five?"

An elegantly dressed man to Melissa's right obliged with a slight raise of his manicured right hand.

Melissa's attention shifted to the telephones installed along one wall to take long-distance bids. Three were occupied; Melissa wondered if there were a madman somewhere on the other end.

Christian gave her a questioning expression, and she answered with a slight shake of her head.

The Charles II cup went for $30,000 and was replaced by, "A Chinese for-export fish bowl, decorated in underglaze blue. Circa 1760. Diameter: twenty-three-and-a-half inches. Shall we start . . ."

The explosion and resulting fireball deafened and blinded. They, also, imploded the line of French windows behind the auctioneering stand and sent shards of glass flying inward in a display of sparkling, far-reaching brilliance that was as beautiful as it was deadly. The kaleidoscope of shattered crystal was accompanied by billowing yellow smoke that quickly formed an eye-stinging fog to hide the screaming victims impaled and bleeding among the first six rows.

"Christian!" Melissa worried about him, not consciously aware airborne glass was the cause of the additional sting and blood along her right forearm.

She couldn't believe she'd somehow lost him, even in a room gone smoky, and din-filled, chairs and people toppled like dominoes. It took someone stepping on her hand for her to realize she wasn't sitting on her chair but lying on the floor.

"Christian!" Her eyes and throat burned, and tears welled up protecting delicate eye-tissue.

When she tried to get to her feet, she cut her palms on the glass-covered floor.

"Christian!" His hands were beneath her arms, lifting her to her feet.

She couldn't really see him. She couldn't see much of anything, but his sheer physicality enabled him to make a way for them where there hadn't been one. He kicked chairs out of their way with a clatter that rearranged the maze.

When the gunfire began, sparkler-like flashes of orange amid the heavy yellow, he jerked her out of the way and put himself between her and any oncoming bullets.

She took hold of his neck, buried her face against his chest, and thought if she just commanded herself to wake up, the nightmare would end.

When the gunfire stopped, Christian proceeded to move them farther from the source of yellow smoke which, somewhere, belched even thicker fog. He could hardly see to put one step in front of the other.

Melissa's view was equally as jaundiced, distorted by her tears. Her lungs protested their inability to absorb the chemically produced gas by refusing to breathe it unless she consciously gasped in air with the irritant.

She stumbled, grabbed for Christian and pulled an invisible something off the wall. It was while Christian helped her to her feet that she realized she'd dislodged books from their shelf; she didn't remember books on her way in. Were they in one of the side rooms?

Somewhere, someone, collided with something that shattered more glass on the floor. Some of those fragments skittered far and wide to collide against her feet.

"There's got to be a window?" Christian said and felt along the books for an access to the outside.

Melissa kept hold of his coat and stumbled behind.

"Window over here!" someone shouted. "Here!"

"Break it!" Christian demanded.

"I can't. My legs!"

Christian took her hand and headed toward the voice. He bumped a table and toppled more unseen artifacts.

"Over here!" their mentor obliged, although he sounded none too good through his coughing.

"Yes!" Melissa exclaimed and spotted a rectangular slice of milky light through tear-distorted, blurry yellow.

Christian picked up a chair. He didn't know it was a chair, only that it was handy. Anything large and not fastened to the floor would have done as nicely. Its momentum carried it through the glass and onto the lawn.

Melissa would have followed immediately after it and the smoke that had rushed to follow, but Christian used a book to hammer down shards left behind to booby-trap the window.

"Now!" he said finally and helped a by-now gagging Melissa up and over the sill.

If Melissa expected immediate respite, she was disappointed. The smoke that had preceded them formed a thick, low-lying pocket to cocoon them.

Their luck, though, improved when they finally came out of it at a garden fountain, complete with Grecian maid pouring from a central position. Christian dropped and brought Melissa to her knees beside him. The impact painfully telescoped her spine. He put his hand behind her head and brought her face forward and down at the same moment he drenched his own head beneath the water in the marble basin. He opened his eyes beneath the water to rinse them and came up for air.

Melissa came up gasping but had sense enough to return, on her own, for more of the same. She dunked twice more before the stinging became bearable.

Christian was the most wondrous sight her reddened eyes could behold. All she wanted was his arms around her, his body against her, his voice in her ear to reassure that everything was all right.

"Wait here!" To her utter amazement, he left her for a return to that world of smoke between them and the house.

"Christian!" She didn't understand. She wanted him with her.

Her selfishness, though, only lasted as long as it took to remember there was someone in there who had guided them to their escape hatch. Someone whose legs, for whatever the reason, had prevented him from breaking the glass himself.

She faced the billowing smoke and demanded it spit Christian back up. She found the sudden ray of sunshine that penetrated mainly overcast sky to illuminate a blaze of nearby red roses perverted; this scenario called for total gloom and doom.

For all outward appearance, she was alone in the yellow smoke filled garden, but she heard injured people not far away, hidden from her by smoke, walls, windows, green lawn, and obscenely red, red roses.

"Melissa!"

It was Christian.

She couldn't see him. Was there no end to the smoke? Why was it yellow? Was there a yellow fire, too? After the initial fireball, she'd seen no sign of flames, but that didn't mean it wasn't there, lurking just a few feet away.

"Melissa!"

He needed her, and right now he was more important to her than life itself.

"I'm coming, Christian! I'm coming!"

Throwing caution to the wind, she reentered the chemical cloud to join the man she loved.

11

The return to that jaundiced world with its irritant that stung her eyes and throat which were already raw and sensitive from first exposure wasn't an experience to savor. Christian's continuing calls for help drew her farther and farther into the morass.

He was at the window, trying to keep the body of an unconscious man precariously balanced on the edge of the sill.

Melissa wiped her eyes to better focus the problem, but all she got were more tears for her efforts.

"Just hold him!" Christian instructed. "He's hung up somewhere on the other side, and I couldn't get to it or he'd fall."

She leaned on the man to anchor him. With her help, Christian got him loose with surprisingly little effort. "Let's move!"

They tugged him over the lip and to the ground. From there, more effort freed him of the low-hanging smoke.

"He's bleeding." Melissa saw that even through her tears.

Christian produced a Swiss army knife and cut lengthwise up the man's pant legs. He peeled back the material to reveal glass-studded flesh.

"He's lucky he got as far as he did!" Christian said with an educated guess. "I'd better find a doctor."

"Where?" For a brief second of insanity, she had a vision of his return to the smoke-filled rooms to ask, "Is there a doctor in the house?"

"Everyone must be out in front." He was off in an instant.

Melissa preferred him close, but she was less fearful for his safety as long as he was outside. If the attackers were who she thought they were, they hadn't stuck around.

The injured man moaned which Melissa decided was a good sign. She ripped a tail from her blouse and soaked it with enough water to wipe his tear-stained face. But she'd probably do more harm than good if she messed with the glass shards in his legs.

His eyes flickered, then opened. They were attractively hazel eyes and made his otherwise normal, dark-complected handsomeness seem quite extraordinary. They remained unfocused while he coughed and made spasmodic efforts to sit, the latter Melissa was able to prevent.

"Someone has gone for a doctor," she encouraged. "It's best you keep as quiet as . . ."

"Medic! Medic! Medic!" he screamed at the top of his lungs. It would have provided results if there were a doctor within miles.

Almost simultaneously, his eyes focused and showed remembrance of things past.

"Sorry," he apologized, although he had to know apologies weren't necessary. "I thought I was back in Nam. Yellow camouflage smoke. Tear gas. Grenades."

"Grenades?"

"Forty mm. I'd guess from a M79 hand-held launcher. I used them in Nam."

"This is Seattle," she reminded him.

"Sounded like 9 mm parabellum sub-machine gun."

"Model 12? Manufacturerer: Pietro Beretta (Italy)?" It just slipped out of her like egg from its shell.

"Hey, we must have had the same teacher." He managed a wan smile. "Uncle Sam exposing women to battle conditions these day?"

"Just some trivia I picked up along the way." She was angry he'd survived Nam to be taken out by a madman after a lousy piece of steel, because she had no doubts who was behind this. If the means seemed drastic for the end, a maniac didn't think the way normal people did.

There were distant sirens that suggested help was on the way. "It won't be long," she said, only to realize he'd slipped back into unconsciousness. Although that spared him pain, she would have preferred him conscious and talking.

She vaguely remembered some kind of vital artery in the leg. Femoral artery: that was it! If she remembered correctly, though, it was somewhere on the inner thigh. Most of his damage seemed from the knees down.

She heard more sirens, but it seemed ages before Christian returned with one of the men they'd met at Volunteer Park; they had a makeshift travois made out of two commandeered fence poles and a blanket; the blanket she'd once seen in the trunk of Christian's car.

"The doctors are pretty busy," Christian said. "Bill and I figured if the mountain won't come to Mohammed . . ."

Bill examined the wounds. "I've seen people come through much worse without major limps." He checked the cuts on her arm and palms. "Yours are just scratches."

Melissa didn't know by what authority he made his prognosis, but he sounded knowledgeable, and she chose to believe him.

They lifted the man on the travois and hauled him around front to a scene of wounded straight out of *Gone With The Wind*. Melissa refused to budge until a doctor assured her the man's wounds were, indeed, less serious than they looked; by then, a hospital evac-helicopter was setting down on the front lawn.

Melissa said to Christian, "He fought in Nam. He recognized grenades, tear gas, yellow camouflage smoke, sub-machine-gun fire. You know what he said when I asked if it might have been Model 12, Beretta? He said, 'We must have had the same teacher.' "

Christian, though, didn't get the connection. He'd not been there when Inspector Dwighton had asked Carol and Melissa about Kevin's last words.

"That's what Kevin said about his killer: 'E.T. forgot we had the same teacher.' "

"The killer and Kevin's same teacher: Uncle Sam?"

"Maybe we should find whomever is in authority, and tell them what we know and suspect."

"The Seattle Police Department isn't going to be any more delighted about a killer with a penchant for outer-space weaponry than the LAPD, or our home-grown Canadian police force," Christian said.

"They're going to have a hard time refuting our theory if the Bearhound Bowie is missing from inside, as a result of all of this, aren't they?"

"If there's any way to avoid it, they'll take any theory but our theory," Christian said. "On the other hand, yes, I think we should give it our best shot."

Sergeant Darla Potter, Seattle Police Department, listened from start to finish without interruption. When they were done, she sent Patrolman Howard Toole to check Lot #1246.

"I'm a little confused." It sounded as if the fault were all hers. "The dying man, Kevin . . ."

She waited for Melissa to fill the blank, "Silner."

". . . identified his killer, through Mae Ling and Sylint, as Captain Steven E.T. Miller. Yet, Captain Miller has been declared legally dead as a result of the same crash that you and Mr. Wynard survived."

"We know there are a lot of unanswered questions," Christian admitted.

"It's certainly the kind of story the press would love." Sgt. Potter didn't sound as if she shared that emotion.

Melissa and Christian exchanged glances that weren't lost on Sgt. Potter.

"Admittedly, it's a theory to which I have all intentions of paying attention," she assured them as if they'd take it to the press if she didn't give it the credence it deserved. "On the other hand, I'd like you to listen to another possibility, and let me know how it plays in Sheboygan."

"Sure." Christian settled back in a chair, in the Tefson mansion pool house that the police used for their interrogations.

"If I eventually put more faith in this potential, it's because we got a confession called in to the main station just awhile ago from a group called *The Friends of Joe Halloey.*"

Melissa had been in Seattle, previewing the gnome-porcelains of Mallin Tinstin at her gallery, when the Joe Halloey story had broken. He'd been a northwest drug kingpin picked up on charges of trafficking illegal substances, perjury before a grand jury, conspiracy to commit murder, murder, and seventy-two other counts. He'd recently been convicted to serve time in some federal facility back east. "You see this as drug-related?"

"Denner Tally was at the auction this afternoon." Since the name obviously wasn't recognized the sergeant explained, "Prosecuting Attorney Denner Tally."

"Killed?" Melissa could imagine the killer willing to murder by way of supplying another red herring to keep everyone guessing.

"Unfortunately for *The Friends of Joe Halloey,* no. However, two bullet holes are going to lay him up for a very long time."

"I'm sorry," Melissa said. However, that didn't mean she believed, for a minute, any of this *really* had anything to do with Joe Halloey and his getting busted for shipping cocaine in from Peru.

"Now, I'm going to be frank," the sergeant admitted, "in that I tend to view all of this . . ." A wave of her hand indicated the catastrophe still not cleared up outside and in the big house. ". . . as financed by Halloey's playmates out for revenge, rather than by a madman on a shopping trip for another knife with which to kill women as instructed by voices from outer space." She somehow made it come out without sounding as if the knife story was *really* all that far-fetched; Melissa wondered how she did it.

"You'll admit there are definite military overtones to this raid, particularly as regards choice of weaponry." Christian knew where this would take him, but he didn't want the police to look back and say he hadn't given them every opportunity.

"Which could support your theory that we're dealing with a madman who served in Nam," Darla was magnanimous. "On the other hand, there are lots of veterans from that war around these days."

Melissa had to agree. There had probably been more than a few at the auction, if the man Christian and she rescued from the building were a good random sample.

"Meaning, without a war to fight, their expertise and services might come cheaply?" Christian said.

"The Halloey organization was, at one time, reported to have moved over sixteen-million dollars of narcotics into the

U.S. every single day." Insinuating that if expertise and services came cheaply, what could *really* big money buy?

Patrolman Toole, sent to check Lot #1246, returned and stood to one side until Darla motioned him in.

"Lot #1246 is missing." He pulled out his note pad to verify the fact.

The sergeant looked genuinely surprised, and Melissa exchanged a triumphant glance with Christian which was diluted by the same messenger.

"The auction staff reports, just from a cursory inspection, that Lot #1245, an emerald ring; 1247, a miniature Russian icon; 1240, A Romanov snuff box; 1260, a pair of Japanese, Arita, 17th-century porcelain boys; and, 1262, a Jon Brogdan brooch, are, also, missing."

"Ah!" Sgt. Potter sounded like a wrestler saved by the bell. "It would seem the Bearhound Bowie becomes one of several artifacts picked up during the excitement by person or persons unknown."

"We've already told you our man has always been clever enough to conceal true intent," Melissa reminded her.

Patrolman Toole, apparently on the same wavelength as his superior, gave the sergeant additional support. "Mr. Grendle says thefts, like these, often occur at times like these."

"Mr. Grendle is an expert on times like these?" Melissa didn't know Mr. Grendle, but she didn't like him.

Patrolman Toole, apparently less able than Sgt. Potter to distinguish sarcasm, took Melissa's query in all seriousness and flipped to another page in his pad. "Mr. Grendle handled the Linlex estate sale when fire broke out in the wiring. Four items were ripped off in the ensuing confusion."

After which, Sgt. Potter remained polite, swore she remained open-minded, but still got across she had been presented by *The Friends of Joe Halloey* with a synopsis that worked; it wasn't likely she'd throw it overboard in favor of a resurrected madman stealing meteorite knives to carve up streetwalkers on command from little green aliens.

It was a possible indication, however, of the exploitive potential of the E.T.-killer theory, that had her not only grant Melissa and Christian leave *not* to stick around for further questioning, but volunteer a police squad car to escort them to the airport.

"After such a trying afternoon, I think we'll stay at The Sorrento until morning." It was true Melissa and his afternoon had been trying, but there was no denying he said what he said to make the sergeant nervous. In truth, he was no more anxious for the papers to get hold of the story than she was. He didn't want the madman scared off by publicity that said the killer lurked just off stage.

"It might be difficult to get hotel reservations." The sergeant's expression said she was sorry for that bit of ridiculousness the minute it passed her lips. She hadn't gotten to where she was without an awareness of how things worked in the big, wide world. Money talked, and Christian Wynard had enough to talk him and Melissa into any hotel, anywhere.

"My company keeps two suites at The Sorrento," he rubbed home the point that he couldn't be so easily dislodged if he set his mind to prevent it.

Sgt. Potter knew when to beat a diplomatic retreat. "You're probably right to put this behind you with a good-night's sleep. If you should think of anything else . . ." She handed him her card with office and home phones.

Melissa and Christian were sure she had already heard more from then than she wanted.

"Well, we did guess how that would go," Christian observed when they were in the limo headed east on Broadway.

"He—whomever *he* might be—certainly knows how to pull the police's strings." The thought of him as expert puppet master gave her an ill-at-ease feeling that only Christian's hug cured.

She was ready to head for bed as soon as they checked into The Sorrento, but she didn't want to wake up at two in the morning; so, she agreed to an early supper with Christian in the hotel's top-floor restaurant. First, she took a long bath that left her so limp she almost cancelled. Then, she called Carol to assure they'd be back for Kevin's memorial and burial.

In the end, she was glad she hadn't gone directly to bed. She needed a few moments of companionable restfulness in order to unwind. A meal with Christian, at a window table that overlooked the Seattle skyline, was just what the doctor ordered. As it got darker, the lights going on and off in city skyscrapers, table candlelight offering a mellow space of intimacy which two people could readily share, it was almost, if not quite, possible to forget why they were there.

"So, I get my spur-of-the-moment trip to Seattle; the man of my dreams; *and* supper by candlelight." She gave him an intimate smile.

She avoided mentioning how naïve they'd been to think the killer would be obliging and let them simply walk into the auction and catch him. Almost as naïve had been their assumption he might send someone to bid on the knife for him. After all, he didn't have a history of acquisitions by legal means. On the other hand, there *had* been the outside chance the knife would go unnoticed on the auction block, and Christian could buy his killer-bait rather than custom-make it.

Christian took her hand, opened her fingers, and kissed her palm where glass cuts had been cleaned by her lengthy bath. He kissed her wrist and, when the waitress asked if he would like dessert, he kissed Melissa's wrist again and said, "Nothing could be this good."

Whether it could or not, they shared a decadently caloric chocolate mousse before surrendering the enchantment to schedule their early-morning departure. Christian would have the plane ready by eight a.m., which would give them plenty of time to make the memorial service at two. Melissa needed another change of clothes. Her suit once fit for tomorrow's services, now had a decidedly acidic smoky smell, was dirty, and was cut in several places. Her supper ensemble, a long skirt with flowered hem, with matching blouse, retrieved from the bag Mrs. Carson had packed, wasn't appropriate for final farewells to Kevin.

Inside her room Christian took Melissa in his arms. A flood of excitement rushed through her when his lips met hers. When they finally separated, she said with a breathless little laugh, "Your kisses are sweeter than chocolate mousse."

"After our luscious dessert tonight, I take that as high praise indeed!" His hands gently circled her face and he whispered, "Sweet dreams, lovely lady."

She expected to sleep the minute her head hit the pillow; so much for expectations. She remained in a suspended state between awake and asleep that bestowed none of the satisfaction of either.

When the phone rang, she answered, "You couldn't sleep, either?" That seemed a natural response, in that so few people, besides Christian, knew she was there.

"In bed already? My, what an evocative picture that presents to someone with my vivid imagination!"

"You!" Melissa pulled her blanket all of the way to her chin and shivered. She'd always known she'd recognize his eyes; just how deeply his voice had embedded in her psyche she hadn't realized until now.

"Ah, you *do* remember!" As if she could very well forget! "I was going to say hello this afternoon, but you and Mr. Wynard, so unexpectedly at the auction, left me literally speechless. I would have been disappointed had either of you been hurt; it's so difficult to work around unexpected arrivals."

"It *was* you!"

"I, or *The Friends of Joe Halloey*. Shall I give you my theory as to whom the police suspect?" His laugh oozed self-satisfaction.

"Call to gloat?" she accused. "Need to brag how clever you think you are?"

"Oh, I don't need to solicit from the likes of you; I have non-stop congratulations incoming from far higher authorities. Actually, I called to do you and your boyfriend a big favor."

"Why did you kill Kevin?" Although she was shaking, while she had him on the line, she wasn't going to pass the opportunity to press for answers.

He wasn't so easily diverted, and he answered her with exaggerated heavy breathing.

"You know that Kevin mistook you for Captain Steven Miller?"

"Yes, I believe I did hear something to that effect."

"So, who are you? Why did you kill Kevin? Why did you kill all those women?"

"Yours is not to reason why; yours is but to do or die." Pure evil rode his voice, like poison into the ears of the king in the play within a play in *Hamlet*.

"Do you look like Captain Miller?"

"You met me. You met Captain Miller. You think we look alike?"

"You wore a mask, but your eyes didn't look anything like his." She wished she hadn't said that. She felt uneasy as if she'd given a secret away.

"Do you have a pencil or pen handy, Melissa? Do you have a scrap of paper on which to write something?"

She groped for something to write with, but before she could find anything, he rattled off an address, and added, "That's in Vancouver, by the way, not here in Seattle."

So, he was still in Seattle. Where, though? She listened for something on his end of the line that would betray his hiding

place. Angela Lansbury, on *Murder She Wrote,* would hear a
church bell, or a passing train, or factory machinery.

Melissa heard a dial tone.

She called Christian.

"Couldn't sleep, either, huh?"

She laughed, almost a hysterical response. "It's kind of hard
to sleep with calls at all hours."

"From me?"

"From the murderer."

"*He* called you."

"He's in Seattle."

"We knew that, didn't we?"

"He had an address for us in Vancouver." She repeated it
from memory. "Mean anything to you?"

"Only that it's a couple blocks east of the warehouse where
my meteorite was stolen. Did he tell you what was there?"

"Only the address."

"Not to meet him there?"

"Just the address."

"You hang up, and I'll call Inspector Dwighton. If the killer
thinks we're trotting there on our own, he's crazy!"

"Think I should call Sgt. Potter?"

"Think it worth the effort?"

"I'd prefer she have all the information, it's her fault if she
doesn't act on it."

"Suit yourself."

She called her. The sergeant sounded tired but remained
polite throughout. When Melissa finished, she thanked her,
wished her a good flight to Vancouver in the morning, and that
was that.

Receiver down, the phone rang again. It was Christian.
"Inspector Dwighton said he'd check the Vancouver address."

Fifteen minutes later, she called Christian back. "It's
hopeless; I can't sleep."

"Neither can I. I'll have the plane made ready for immediate takeoff."

An hour later, the lights of SEATAC were lost in the low-lying fog behind them.

Less than an hour after that, they were in Vancouver.

Despite the late hour, Mrs. Carson and Inspector Dwighton were there to meet them.

"I called The Sorrento," explained Mrs. Carson. "The front desk said you'd both just checked out."

"I did too," explained Dwighton.

Mrs. Carson handed over a manilla envelope which had been hand-delivered by Toby late that evening.

"Take tomorrow off," Christian told her, tucked the envelope under his arm, and turned his attention to Inspector Dwighton.

The inspector had an envelope of his own, produced from the inside pocket of his suit coat. He peeled back the flap and spilled out two photographs which he turned over to Christian as Melissa looked on.

"Oh!" Melissa exclaimed; the photos were not pretty.

"Do you know either of those people?" The inspector must have known it would be difficult to tell. "Until earlier this evening, they were merely another John and Jane Doe, discovered in a ditch by a passing motorist. They're comatose at Vancouver General, long-range prognosis not good."

"Is there any reason we should know them?" Christian handed the pictures back, disgusted the inspector had subjected Melissa to the sight.

"Does Helen duPlay and Roger Cantrell ring any bells?"

Melissa shook her head.

"Not for me, either," Christian said after some thought.

"They were students in a study group Elizabeth Howard taught at the University of British Columbia."

"I'm not sure what this has to do with us," Christian said.

The inspector produced two more photographs from the same envelope.

Melissa was relieved these were simple passport photos of a young blond man and a young blonde woman. She thought she was seeing the before of before-and-after pictures; she was wrong.

"Silvia Petre and Alan Westchester," the inspector identified.

"Who are they?" Christian said.

The inspector, though, apparently wasn't to be hurried. "Two more members of that same study group, these two . . ." He tapped the passport pictures. ". . . we apprehended at the address you called in from Seattle."

"I'm afraid I still don't . . ."

Melissa, though was quicker. "Roger Cantrell, Alan Westchester: Roger, Alan: the two I heard mentioned during the scuffle when the meteorite was stolen?" ·

"Very good!" the inspector said. "Alan has a very nasty bite on his arm."

"They're the ones who took the meteorite!" Christian exclaimed.

"As the meteorite, now recovered, would seem to indicate."

When Christian wasn't exuberant, Melissa concluded there was a problem.

"Do you want me to come out with what you're thinking, or do I spill the incredible?" Christian said.

"You do see, then, how circumstantial evidence . . ."

"Melissa and I were in Seattle!" Christian interrupted him.

"You have money. Things can be bought."

"What's he talking about?" Melissa said.

"That I figured out how some of Elizabeth's students absconded with my property, which they figured belonged to their beloved, martyred teacher. That I hired a thug to persuade them to confess to the deed."

"That's crazy!" Melissa said outraged. She turned her full fury on the inspector. "Didn't Christian tell you who called *me* with that address?"

"Kevin's killer? Or, was it the resurrected Captain Miller?"

"It's true!" Melissa insisted, although not even she was sure how much.

"It's *convenient!*" the inspector put forth his own definition. "Wynard has his meteorite back in the guise of further verification that there's a killer with a penchant for meteorite knives. Why else would this madman oblige by personally seeking out the stolen meteorite if he didn't hope your boyfriend would reward him with a new knife for his collection?"

"Exactly!" Melissa was glad the inspector had come around to their way of thinking, except . . .

"The inspector actually *prefers* the other explanation," Christian said. "He's leery of anything that smacks of a serial killer with a 'thing' for weapons made of meteorite metal. His is the always present fear that the press will make a fool out of him if he goes for anything offbeat, isn't it inspector? It's far easier to believe I hired someone to beat two college kids comatose to get back my stolen property?"

The inspector looked uneasy, and Melissa thought he had every right to. What he hinted was ridiculous!

"I have to look at all options," the inspector said.

"You're an ostrich with your head in the sand!" Melissa said, not bothering to be diplomatic. "I only hope, for all our sakes, you pull it out one day soon."

"We'll see what Helen and Roger say when, or if, they regain consciousness." The inspector made it a warning.

"If you're not finished with us, we're finished with you!" Christian abruptly informed him.

"Don't leave town next time without letting me know first." Apparently the inspector wanted the last word.

Christian wouldn't oblige him. "Someone will contact you

about the paperwork required to get back my property. If you have anything else to say, contact Tendram Cruz of Cruz, Sills, Macternac and Todd."

Taking Melissa's arm, he guided her through the door by which Mrs. Carson had exited earlier.

The full effect of the inspector's suspicions didn't strike Melissa, until she climbed into the car, then she started shivering uncontrollably. Christian pulled her closer for reassuring comfort.

"I can't believe he believes you had anything to do with that!" she said when she had calmed down slightly.

"The man is a cop!" Christian didn't make it a compliment. "Sgt. Potter would have reached the same conclusion, a country away, as Dwighton reached here. It's so much easier to believe a military operation for revenge of an arrested drug kingpin, an artist killed during a drug buy, two kids pounded senseless because a rich man gets ticked off about pilfered property. They want neat little packages, done up in bright red ribbons. They *don't* want a madman getting messages from extra-terrestrials to hand-pick meteorite knives for murder; especially not if the killer is clever enough to play on every cop's paranoia about the press."

Melissa's chills stopped, replaced by pure, unadulterated anger. "The man's a fool! So is Sgt. Potter!"

Christian was more magnanimous. "It's the nature of overworked, underpayed, public servants to be wary of a press that has, rightly or wrongly, burned them once too often in the past."

He gave Melissa another hug: "Feel warmer?"

"The real question: will I ever get warm again?"

"Take a look at this . . ." He handed her the manilla envelope from Toby that Mrs. Carson had delivered. ". . . and give me an idea of the contents while I drive." He retrieved the flashlight, back under the seat after its outing in the basement of the burned-out building.

Melissa switched on the light and unsealed the envelope. Christian started the car and entered it into traffic far less hectic, at that late hour, than it had been when they'd made the trip in.

Melissa found interesting reading. "It says here that Miller was the key man in a mess-up in Nam that included foul-ups by some very high-ranking officers." One of the names—Kenteth, a colonel at the time—rang a bell as the man who had more recently ordered the cremation of Miller's body. "Seems a special-forces unit was ordered into Cambodia when U.S. troops weren't supposed to be in Cambodia; there to 'take out' a village thought to be a Cong supply depot but, only afterwards, found not to be one.

"On the way back, Miller's group was put under 'friendly' fire by some very nervous U.S. top brass out to dispose of eyewitnesses to their Cambodian debacle. Miller's sole survival of Cambodia *and* the friendly fire made him a time bomb waiting to go off and ruin some high-ranking military men's credibility and careers, even if he were rumored a little brain-scrambled by the ordeal.

"A true glimpse of his devious character was how he didn't turn in those who did everything but put him in an early grave; he set up a lucrative drug and black-market operation under their largesse. The illegal profits were pumped into his pockets right up until the fall of Saigon.

"Back in the States, he continued to milk his contacts for protection for various shady deals."

Christian flashed Melissa a meaningful glance. "Ergo: lots of enemies in the making, right?"

"It does come across here that he was an accident waiting to happen, especially after some apparently nasty, but still-under-wraps something happened when he was stationed at Wycoff outside of Chicago. After which, he was shipped to Ft. Lewis outside Seattle where, at his own request, and with help from some 'friends' anxious to give him a badly needed low profile, he was assigned to pilot the helicopter on loan to CanTech."

"None of which some people figured would make interesting listening on the five-o'clock news." Christian saw the logic: soldiers were experts at killing; the bomb or bombs that killed the captain had been specifically placed to take him out. A military hierarchy, anxious to keep its image squeaky clean, wouldn't like what the press might make with all of that.

"Seems, then, there's a good chance Miller was bumped off by one or more of his own kind within the military superstructure?" She'd made it a question but she knew what the facts said. "The captain was an opportunistic sleaze, possibly more than a little crazy, with enemies and one-time-friends-now-enemies from Saigon to Seattle; anyone of whom might have followed him into Canada to blow him away. No wonder, the military and CanTech decided on a cover-up that included not coming after you and lying to make Miller's death seem an accident."

She tried to remember Captain Miller. He'd seemed distant and military: that was about the extent of her recall.

She was about to put the documents back when hand-written notations, "NO PICTURE!", on several pages caught her attention.

"Toby apparently had trouble locating a picture of Miller. Pages that obviously once had a picture attached, no longer have one."

Christian picked up the phone and got hold of Toby within minutes. "Yes, just scanned them. Good job, except why no picture? Rather strange if they were pulled everywhere. Maybe a concentrated effort, but surely one, somewhere, slipped through the net."

He hung up and smiled reassuringly. "He's still working on a picture."

Melissa sat back, shut her eyes, and marveled how so much had happened in so short a time. She felt as if she'd been on a roller coaster ride and right now she wondered if she'd ever get off. All because she'd innocently agreed to help Elizabeth find a meteorite, she'd been in a helicopter crash, kidnapped, attempted murder, murder, a shooting gallery, and not the last of which was love for Christian. Amazing and wonderful!

Her life, as a mere gallery owner, out to make ends meet and clear a little profit, seemed far removed from the woman crashed in a helicopter, dumped over a waterfall, and machine-gunned in a hospital.

She dozed and woke with the aftertaste of dreams not remembered. Her eyes focused on a street sign: Howe. The penthouse wasn't far. "I fell asleep."

"Next, you'll tell me it was the company." His gentle chiding was rife with humor.

"Not a chance!" She stretched in a small space available and, in doing so, touched his cheek with her hand, just for the pure pleasure of the touching.

They parked outside the penthouse building.

"Want to come in?" Would she ever get her fill of him? She was sorry now she'd slept most of the way in.

"I think one of us disturbing Carol will be enough. Tomorrow isn't going to be easy on her, what with her parents in town, the memorial service, and the burial."

Actually, Carol seemed to have everything in hand. "Mom and dad got in late yesterday," she told Melissa over breakfast. "I put them up at my place. Memorial at two. A little something will be said at the grave."

"How are your parents taking it?"

"Kevin hadn't let them be much in his life for years. I think they officially laid their son to rest a long time ago. Now they can be completely at peace knowing at last he is."

Melissa headed to her condo. She picked up her mail and a

new set of keys from the manager. He prepared her for the surprise of not having to face the wreckage of the last time. "Did a right fine job," he commended. "Wouldn't know the mess it was once in."

"Who?"

"The painters and such that Mr. Wynard sent around. I hope it was okay to let them in."

More than okay! Even the smell of Shalimar had miraculously been exorcised from the air.

"Oh Christian, I love you!" she said after she'd opened the door on newly painted walls, furniture righted, drapes exactly duplicated but obviously new. The leg of her harewood console had been repaired by an expert; it was impossible to see where it had snapped off. The one-time gouge in the wall was camouflaged with new plaster and painted over. The cause of that now-invisible damage, *The Neputine Brig on the Rocks at Point Hatteras,* was on an end table where she thought she actually preferred it. Her bed was made, the oil painting squared away, and a new bottle of Shalimar centered her vanity.

Even the outside weather obliged with rare sunshine to fill the rooms. The total effect made her think she might be able to return here, rather than house-hunt elsewhere. It was a decision that would have to be made, but, as long as John made the penthouse available for a few more days, she'd wait to make it.

Her closets revealed clothes dry-cleaned and still wrapped in plastic. It was an additionally thoughtful touch.

He picked her up at the penthouse at one-thirty and, as she expected he would, waved off his good deeds as really no big deal.

Melissa was surprised by the memorial turnout. The place was packed with people, most of whom looked as if they'd seen better days and probably had.

"It seems Kevin lent most of them money," Carol said,

obviously as surprised as Melissa by the numbers. "Several even thought it time to pay him back." She opened her purse which was stuffed full of envelopes and cash.

The graveyard service was simple, as promised. After which, Carol took her parents directly to the airport to see them off on the next flight.

Christian led Melissa not to his car but to John's.

"We've scheduled you for a quick check-up at the clinic," John said and opened the door. "Although, you look marvelous to me."

She hesitated. "And Christian's physical?"

"Had this very morning," John assured her with a smile.

Christian would have laughed at having anticipated that very question, but the graveyard setting didn't encourage levity. "I'm picking you and John up for an early supper after I take care of a bit of long-overdue paperwork at the office. Carol will join us as soon as her parents are safely airborne."

"Well, it does seem as if everything has been decided." She got in, let Christian shut the door, and she rolled down the window to accept and return his kiss.

"Maybe we should be thinking a double wedding," John suggested as his car joined the last of the cars out of the graveyard.

"Christian hasn't mentioned marriage." Melissa said primly.

"He will," John assured. "Take that as gospel from someone who's known him a very long time."

"And do I assume you've proposed to Carol?"

"I will," John assured. "Take that as gospel from someone who's known me for a very long time. Of course, it might take Carol a little while to realize just how smitten I am with her."

Changing the subject, Melissa said, "Carol says you've suggested plastic surgery."

"A couple of her cuts are deeper than the others. Not much of a scarring, in any case, but why walk around with *any* reminder?"

"General practice, Plastic surgery. Are there any ends to your talents?"

They headed northwest on Highway Seven.

"I always enjoyed general practice the most," John said. "Plastic surgery, though, is enticing with all its attending dollar signs. The Feaswell Clinic, is built on nose-jobs and tummy-tucks!"

He laughed; she laughed, too.

"It's also a taskmaster. If I don't make it a specific point to treat friends, I can be monopolized by oceans of paperwork that make me forget doctoring is what I always wanted my life to be all about. So, you see what a favor you do every time you let me utilize me doctoring skills."

"Exactly!"

As they neared his office, the Vancouver skyline thickened in the distance. The full parking lot at the clinic intimated a booming business. John's private parking space was in the reserved section of the covered garage.

He came around to open the door for Melissa, and she slid out.

"Well, isn't this a pleasant surprise!" exclaimed an all-too-familiar and chilling voice from nearby shadows.

Melissa whirled to face *him*; his face, except for his reptilian eyes, was sacked by black wool; his right arm was extended with a Beretta M51 aimed in their direction.

12

He ordered them back into the car.

"Much better," he said when he had them in the front seat and he'd assumed his ever-popular, down-in-the-back scrunch.

"What do you want this time?" Melissa asked and tried to keep the tremor out of her voice.

"This comes as no surprise to you, I'm sure, but I've genuinely taken a fancy to this notion of your boyfriend to make a new knife out of meteorite. Of course, I early-on perceived it was a booby-trap for me, but that only enhanced my interest. What I propose, and what I expect you to repeat verbatim, Miss Jordan, is how I'm prepared to deal Wynard's dear friend, Dr. Feaswell, for that contemplated meteorite knife in its finished form."

John was aghast. "You're doing this for a knife?"

"Miss Jordan has possibly already told you what trouble I went to in Seattle for one not nearly as interesting. I now think it only fair that I get not only the knife proposed by Melissa's boyfriend but the one I left behind in Kevin. I was quite fond of the latter knife, and I'll never forgive Kevin for surprising me with all he'd retained from his military self-defense courses. He quite gave an initial impression that drugs had sapped the very last of his strength and coordination. My mistake, and one for which I paid dearly by running short on time and having to leave my knife behind."

"The police have it," Melissa reminded. "You don't think they'll turn it over, do you?"

"Of course, I do. I have all manner of persuasion. For instance, what if I should notify the press about all the murders, here, in L.A., and elsewhere, all committed by knives made from outer-space metal, only a very few ever linked up by the ignorant police?"

"Elsewhere?" That was the word that stuck!

"Surely that doesn't surprise you. After all, I've traveled the world."

John reached his own conclusion: "Stark-raving mad!"

"Not the sort of epitaph to endear you to me during the time you and I shall be spending together," came the none-too-friendly reply. "Which brings me to persuasive argument number two in my dealings with the police for their cooperation: I'll offer to provide them with one very dead John Feaswell. What do you suppose the press would do if it were learned the cops could have saved this oh-so-prominent and respected physician?"

Melissa's teeth clicked as shivers rushed her. She remembered his eyes, cold and bereft of compassion. She heard his voice, mocking and full of malice. She sensed his presence, malevolent and evil, just a few inches away from her. The combined effect unnerved and nauseated her.

"The Nova Scotia meteorite is evidence in a theft and two beatings," she said, stalling for time. "Do you forget the condition in which you left Helen duPlay and Roger Cantrell?"

"You must admit their condition produced results," he argued. "Any idiot, with a modicum of sense, could have figured out those sophomoric kids, as worshipful of Elizabeth as they were, ripped off the meteorite in her memory. Getting a confession was merely a matter of applying tried-and-proven methods of interrogation."

"What if they *hadn't* stolen it?" Melissa persisted. If she kept him talking, maybe she or John could think of something.

"Didn't I tell you, it was only *too* obvious they did. Even the police, slow-witted as they are, would have reached that conclusion eventually. Although, I truly doubt they would have made as much out of it as I did."

"Why did you kill Kevin?" It confused her all the more after she'd decided that this man wasn't the one who'd piloted the downed helicopter.

"You would do well to remember, Melissa, that curiosity did, indeed, kill the cat. Satisfaction, despite any ongoing misconceptions, did *not* bring him back. Now, we've wasted far too much time with this little chat. So, kindly exit the car and wait fifteen minutes after we leave before you deliver my demands to your boyfriend and the police, in whichever order your little heart prefers."

"You won't get away with this?" John had again found his tongue.

"Of course, I will!" their antagonist protested. "I've a coterie of advisers to put you and the stupid cops to shame."

"Extraterrestrials?" Even as she asked, she knew it was Captain Miller who had supposedly heard voices from outer space, and this man and that dead pilot were not one and the same. Nevertheless, she sensed a connection — somewhere.

His laugh was not condusive to good cheer. "Extraterrestrials? Oh, by all means! And won't the press, along with everything else, go ape over that notion? Do, Melissa, drop that little jewel in some newspaperman's ear and see the police thank you." He laughed again.

"John?" She turned to him, helpless as to how to help him, and a feeling of guilt that she was glad that madman wasn't taking her with him this time.

"It'll be okay, Melissa." It was a stock reassurance that Melissa didn't believe.

"One final thing, Melissa," came the voice from the back. "I can't tell you how pleased I'd be if you designed the handle for this knife that Christian will be making for me. I presume he or you has already suggested that possibility?"

"No!" But it had only been a matter of time, and she knew it. She'd already sketched several design ideas for the handle on bond paper found in the penthouse secretaire.

"Well, I'm suggesting it. I rather fancy a daughter-son collaboration as a companion piece to the father-father knife I still have in my collection, and the father-father knife the police will soon return to me."

"They *won't,* you know!"

"Well, I won't be as stingy in returning Dr. Feaswell if they don't. Now, get out!"

"John?" What did she expect of John when she was so helpless?

"Do as he says, Melissa."

"Excellent suggestion!" the man in back confirmed.

She got out and looked around for help. So many cars, but no people!

John started the car and pulled it out of the parking spot. He managed a grin smile and wave as he drove by.

Melissa glanced where her wristwatch would have been if it had survived the crash landing of the helicopter, which it hadn't. So, how did she tell fifteen minutes? One-thousand, one-thousand-one . . .

Counting didn't work. She kept losing track. She kept rehashing what had just happened. She kept trying to find the moment when she might have turned the tables and taken control. She was frustrated how *he* always seemed so much in control. Maybe he did get his smarts from little green men. Except, it was Captain Miller in touch with aliens, and he was dead. So, why had Kevin sworn him resurrected? Where *was* the interconnecting link?

She called Christian from one of the pay phones in the reception area of the clinic. She took a cab to the penthouse to meet him.

He looked worried. He knew what kind of crazy they dealt with: Helen duPlay had just died at Vancouver General without having regained consciousness.

Melissa called Inspector Dwighton who told her and Christian to stay put; he'd be right over.

While she waited, Melissa removed her sketches from the drawer of the secretaire and brought them to Christian.

"What are these?" He knew what they were; even as he'd asked, he'd shaken his head.

"They're rough, I know, but you get the idea of how they'd look in scrimshaw on fossilized mastadon ivory, or on whatever else you might prefer for the handle of this knife of yours."

"I don't want you involved any deeper."

"Too late! By coincidence by fate, I've been involved from the start. I drew these even before that madman suggested I do the handle. It was something I wanted to do, and it's now something I have to do. It'll give us a bargaining chip he can't resist. If he wants it badly enough, he'll keep John safe for the trade. Oh, Christian . . ."

"How I do adore you."

"Pick!" She nodded to the selection.

"This one." It was waterfall, rocks, startled bear; a fireball descended through burning pines.

"Now, put your arms around this woman you love, because she is suddenly very, very cold!"

* * *

The police desperately sought a way out. With Helen duPlay's death, the meteorite had become material evidence in her murder, just as the Wynard/Jordan knife was evidence in the Kevin Silner homicide.

The madman, though, wasn't pleased or impressed by their attempts at procrastination. He hung up on their bemoanings as to why it couldn't be done, and he called a newspaper. Within minutes, that paper had a reporter on line to Inspector Dwighton with tantalizing key words, like serial murders, outer space, police incompetence, cover-up kidnappings; all fed by the killer, without specifics.

The police were far more cooperative when the killer got back to them. They assured that steps were being taken to comply with his demands.

Melissa and Christian began work on their part of the ransom. They did so in the blacksmith shed used by Christian's father on the wooded Wynard estate outside Vancouver. The outbuilding, connected to the main house by an underground tunnel, had been ready and waiting, previously renovated by Christian who had always planned to use it; he'd lately practiced regularly to refamiliarize himself with tools he'd long-ago mastered under the tutelage of his father.

Melissa brought her materials and tools from her small studio adjacent to her Gastown gallery. There were tools she might have used in the small soundproof room Kyle Wynard had built off the blacksmith shed for the use of artisans he'd, at times, felt needed to be handy for closer collaborations, but Melissa preferred the familiarity of her own things. She, also, preferred a workbench right in the smithing area, rather than hidden away in the room constructed to be inconspicuous and preserve the integrity of the shed's otherwise rustic, turn-of-the-century flavor.

For Melissa, the artisan's room seemed too totally removed from the knife-making process, and its soundproofing, although an intercom system could be activated to allow the hammer-against-anvil sounds, tended to isolate it even farther. Rather than find that watching and hearing Christian and his activites disturbed her concentration, she found they added genuine inspiration. Ironically, and a bit sad, under the circumstances, her present efforts were beginning to show all signs of being her very best work ever.

With a magnifying glass, she checked her work etched, thus far, on aged-to-pale-amber ivory cut from the tusk of a long-dead mastadon that had been preserved, until recent thaw, within the permafrost of Russian Siberia. The material was her choice over other equally exotic matrix.

She'd smoothed her ivory with 150-, 220-, 400-, and 600-grit sandpaper, followed by rigorous buffing. She'd used a common pencil eraser to prepare the surface for her graphite drawing, much as she'd use the same eraser on greeting cards whose backs were originally too slick to take the ink of a handwritten message spilled over from the inside. After her drawing was finished, she'd preserved it against smear with a coating of acrylic spray. Her scrimshaw tools cut through the acrylic, the graphite, and the polished-to-waterproof surface to gouge the porous layers below. Her coloring, then, permanently dyed the sides and bottoms of her carefully prepared scratches but wiped clean from the acrylic and the highly polished surface. When the carving was finally done, with all its ink applied, the acrylic and remaining graphite would come free with an application of nail-polish remover, followed by a wash in soapy water.

Melissa looked up as Carol entered through the tunnel from the house. Both women and Christian had moved to the estate to save the bother of daily commuting from Vancouver.

Carol leaned close to Melissa in order to be heard over the rhythm of Christian's steady hammer-falls against iron converting to steel. "This just came by special courier." She indicated the envelope in hand.

Christian noticed Carol's presence, and he stopped hammering. His face and arms were highlighted by the veneer of sweat coaxed from his pores by physical exertion and exposure to the heat of the forge. "More word from the madman?"

John's kidnapper had been suspiciously silent after his last of a whole series of telephone discussions with the police, during which he'd mapped out the explicit details of how and where the exchange of weapons for doctor was to take place in exactly two weeks.

"Maybe," Carol admitted without conviction. The man who had kidnapped the man she loved, and she worried more about John for having been there before him, obviously preferred the telephone to written messages.

Christian joined them and opened the envelope. He pulled out the enclosed photo and put it on the workbench.

"It's he!" Melissa exclaimed. She'd know his eyes anywhere, even on the unmasked face in the photo.

"It's, also, Captain Steven E.T. Miller," Christian said, reading the sheet of paper Toby had included with the photo.

"How?" Melissa remained confused. "You saw our pilot. He looked nothing like the man in this picture."

"I'd say Captain Miller has no end to his feats of illusion."

"Someone else died in his place?" Melissa's mind whirled at the prospects such a preplanned substitution would have for making so many pieces suddenly click into place.

"I say we ask him ourselves," Christian suggested. "Because this picture tells us far more than how Captain Miller didn't die, or even didn't go down on that helicopter. It tells us we can expect a visit from him, right here, long before he meets with the police to exchange knives for John — if he ever did plan to meet them and go through with the exchange."

"What makes you think he'll come here?" Carol asked.

Melissa saw. "The photo is another loose end, isn't it? If we've located a photograph that escaped all his attempts to pull them, there are probably more around for other people to find."

Christian winked congratulations. "It's not just the photograph, either," he said mainly for Carol's benefit. "It's a combination of other loose ends, all lying around to spoil his carefully engineered disappearing act."

"Mae Ling, still alive, who Kevin told that Miller was alive," Melissa filled in. "Lenny Sylint who Kevin told that Miller was alive and who Miller tried to have killed but didn't succeed."

"Melissa Jordan who talked to Sylint and heard Miller was alive," Christian reminded.

The list went on and on. "Then, there's the people Miller probably hired to help him in his attempts to kill Sylint, track down Mae Ling, steal the knife in Seattle, and interrogatge Helen duPlay and Roger Cantrell: more than one of whom has probably seen him without his face mask."

"He wanted to drop out of sight," Christian said. "Somehow, he had someone substitute for him in that helicopter, and, when Miller, himself, blew up chopper and pilot, he thought everyone would assume it was he who was dead and gone. Except, it hasn't worked that way, and he's got those enemies made in Nam, in the States, in the drug world, and who knows in where else; any one of whom could be just as clever as we are in figuring out he isn't dead."

Carol obviously wasn't made happier by the insight. "You're suggesting he never intended to trade John for knives. It's somehow another trick to camouflage his real intentions, right?"

"We all know how good he's been at camouflaging intentions, always being sure to take more knives, or more something, to cover his theft of a specific meteorite knife."

"He doesn't want John as a hostage," Carol put the horrible

reality into words. "He wants him for his skills as a plastic surgeon!"

"Captain E.T. Miller, it seems, is out to disappear yet again," Christian gave his agreement to what she suspected.

"He'll have a new face this time," Melissa spelled it out farther.

"Oh!" Carol exclaimed; Christian helped her into a chair. "He won't leave John alive to tell the tale, will he?"

"But we've still a chance," Christian encouraged, "because he *does* have an unnatural, irrational passion for meteorite knives, and he's lost two from his collection, neither of which it now appears likely he'll get back. Even if we count the knife he picked up in Seattle, he's short one."

"He'll come for this one?" Carol's voice was full of hope.

"Yes, I think he will."

"He won't think we're expecting him," Melissa said, "because we're supposedly too distracted by the scheduled exchange of John for two knives in two weeks. *Everything* at this end, he'll figure, is geared toward that date, even the police occupied with how to put something over on him during the exchange."

"What do *we* do?" Carol asked.

"We prepare a surprise welcome for Captain Miller, back from the dead," Melissa put Christian's exact thoughts into words.

Captain Steven E.T. Miller, his face mask on, and his Beretta M51 pistol in hand, came eight days later. His timing, as he must have seen it, was perfect; Melissa had just washed off the last of the acrylic and graphite from the ivory handle, and Christian was performing the last buffing of the blade before uniting ivory and steel into the final, deadly but exquisitely beautiful product.

"Aha!" Melissa greeted, surprised but not *surprised.* Was he clever enough to discern the difference?

Christian turned off the buffer and held up the blade whose highly polished surface caught the light and reflected it. "What do you think?"

Steven was clever, all right. "I think you don't seem particularly surprised to see me."

"We're *not* surprised, Captain Miller," Melissa confessed.

"Captain Miller?"

Did she detect just a bit less certainty in his voice.

"You might as well take off that ridiculous stocking mask," Melissa instructed. "We know who's behind it. We know you didn't go down with that helicopter."

"Got some sucker to stand in for you, didn't you, Miller?" Christian said.

"You've got it all wrong!" He wouldn't have convinced anyone of his innocence.

"Come on, Miller!" Christian said. "This is the final scene of the movie, the last chapter of the book, the place where the villain is confronted and spills his guts, because everyone wants answers, and he's the only one with some of them."

"What makes you think I'm Miller?" He remained noncommittal.

"Kevin dead because he spotted you alive in the bar. Elizabeth Howard dead because you tried to kill Melissa who you thought Kevin had told he saw you alive in the bar. One of your Nam Raider henchmen with a nasty lump on his head because Lenny Sylint, who Kevin told he'd seen you alive in the bar, was quicker at karate than his supposed assassin. Evidence the helicopter was specifically rigged to take out the pilot. Need I go on?"

"Don't forget his picture." Melissa nodded toward the incriminating envelope propped at the back of her workbench.

"Why don't you show him?" Christian suggested. "He's busy

with his gun."

Steven glanced nervously around the work area.

"Look familiar?" Melissa shook his photograph to divert his attention, like a bullfighter flashed red cape before the maddened bull. "Recognize this deadly snake when you see him? It's a picture of Captain Miller who definitely was *not* the pilot of the downed chopper."

"So, where are the police?" he asked suspiciously. "I've cased this place thoroughly for days with no sign of them. You telling me this room is bugged?"

"Melissa and I didn't trust the cops to handle this. They don't want to believe there's a crazy like you running around."

"So, who was the poor guy who took the fall for you, Miller?" Melissa asked.

There was a glazed expression to his eyes that reminded her of Kevin that day at the clinic, and of Lenny in that basement stronghold. This, though, she sensed had nothing whatsoever to do with chemical dependence.

His eyes focused, like a yogi coming out of a meditative trance. His smile hinted a communion with inner voices that had assured him all was well.

He peeled off his mask and revealed an older version of the face in the photo. His short-cropped black hair, regular features, square jaw, cleft chin, high forehead, and full lips, might have come together into an attractive whole, if not for his dead, emotionless, cold, fish-like eyes. "The sacrificial lamb was Lieutenant Ralph Lester." He ran his free hand through his hair and over his face to clear the aftereffects of the confining mask. "An ex-marine-and-helicopter pilot who owed me a favor and was anxious to get out of my debt. Perfect in that the fools at CanTech didn't know a fake me when they saw one. They just ordered one warm body, and that's what I gave them. It helped that he was a loner who hadn't contacted his family since his discharge from the service. It helped that he had my basic complexion and build."

"You wanted a convenient way out of the army, no questions asked," Melissa encouraged, "and a body-double seemed the perfect solution at the time. It had simply gotten too hot for you alive. Not only did you have too many enemies in the service, but . . ." She summoned her recollection of Toby's first, pictureless report. ". . . you'd had some kind of trouble in Chicago when you were stationed at Wycoff."

"A knifing," Steven filled in the blank. "I miscalculated; my victim was lucky, but only to a point; civil authorities were almost at my door when I finagled my transfer to CanTech through Ft. Lewis. There were some top military brass worried that I'd get tracked down on that civil charge to open the even bigger can of worms."

"Meaning your illegal drug activities safely shielded beneath the U.S.-military umbrella all these years." Christian didn't make it a question, and Steven didn't bother to confirm or deny.

"That my fake death screwed up Elizabeth Howard's project was frosting on the cake. My advisers don't approve of meteorites for science."

"You mean your 'voices' don't approve?" Melissa said.

Steven just smiled.

"What do your voices tell you about me, Miller?" Christian asked.

"That you're an important armorer put here specifically to make a weapon I need for ritual sacrifice.

"I thought there was something dreadfully wrong when a knife-maker ended up on the helicopter gone down. I thought they wouldn't have let that happen. Except, they knew that you'd come out alive, only Lester died, as it was supposed to be."

"Did your voices tell you to kill my father?"

"An unfortunate accident. He came home unexpectedly, didn't he? They thought it most unfortunate, too, but they reminded me he'd left a son to follow in his footsteps. We've been waiting a long time for you to make your contribution."

Christian turned the blade so its burnished surface continued to catch the available light and telegraph brilliant flashes. "Do they approve of your intentions to kill me now?"

"They say it's necessary."

"Do they say it's necessary to kill John, too, after he gives you a new identity?"

He seemed genuinely surprised by Christian's insight, as if his whispering voices hadn't warned him beforehand.

"Where's John?" Melissa asked.

"Safe," Steven assured them. "Which is more than I can say for you two."

"Wrong!" Carol said. She'd silently exited the artisans' room where she'd listened on the intercom.

"Who?" He turned as she brought down the barrel of her pistol against the side of his head.

His gun dropped, and he went down on both knees. Melissa scrambled for his weapon. Christian moved fast to make sure Steven wouldn't cause any mischief to force Carol to do further damage.

"You hurt me!" Steven's hands were on his injured head.

"Not nearly as much as I'd like to!" Carol's hands were shaking, and Melissa was afraid her gun might go off accidentally.

On the other hand, Steven wasn't someone to be given any advantage, so it was only after he was securely bound to a chair that Christian took Carol's gun and laid it off to one side.

"You don't know how close I came to pulling the trigger."

"That wouldn't have helped us find John," Christian reminded her.

"You think he's going to tell us where John is?"

"Yes, do you think I am?" Steven's voice was mocking; his eyes were lifeless.

"Do you see John as a bargaining chip?" Christian asked. "Is that what your voices tell you?"

Steven looked uncertain. "Maybe."

"Well, listen very carefully to what they have to say," Christian instructed him. "Because you're going to need every little bit of advice they can give over these next few minutes of your very miserable life."

Christian spent the next few minutes skillfully attaching the ivory handle to the knife tang. When he was through, he showed Steven the results. "Exceptional workmanship if I do say so."

For the very first time, Melissa saw something alive in Steven's eyes: pure, unadulterated lust for an inanimate object; it gave her the shivery creeps.

"Carol?" Christian handed her the knife; Steven's eyes followed the transfer.

"Christian and I are going to leave you two, Captain," Melissa said and moved beside Christian to take his arm. "Carol wants to ask you a few questions in private."

Carol turned the knife edge upward.

Melissa and Christian headed for the door.

"No!" Steven protested.

"Think Carol might take less care in cutting you than you did in cutting her?" Christian stopped and turned back.

"I can't tell you where he is," Steven argued. "They tell me he's the only ace in the hole I have for dealing with the police."

"You better tell them your main concern is dealing with us, right here and now, because this may never get as far as the police."

"After all, Captain Steven Miller is *already* legally dead," Melissa reminded.

Again, Melissa and Christian headed out; again Steven stopped them.

"Please!" It was a pitiful whine.

They turned to see Carol standing very close to him. She'd sliced off two of his shirt buttons, and she had the knife blade resting directly across his jugular vein. It could all be over if Carol let slip. Melissa was deathly afraid they'd come too far. No matter what she'd suggested to him, there was no way she could condone cold-blooded murder, even of this cold-blooded killer.

"I'll tell you!" he said. Then he revealed John's hiding place.

Melissa breathed an audible sigh of relief and welcomed the return of sanity to Carol's eyes.

Christian called in the address to Toby and asked Steven, "How many men do you have guarding him?"

Steven looked at the knife that Carol turned over and over in her hand. He seemed fascinated by the hypnotic effect of light flashing polished steel. "Three," he said, "all well-armed and well-qualified."

Christian passed. on the specifics and hung up. "Toby will call us back when he was him."

"John had better be safe!" Carol warned and pointed the knife in Steven's direction.

The effect was electric. He went rigid and began to shake violently.

"Nooooooo, don't leave me alone!" His voice was little-boy lost and breeching. "It's not my fault! It's *your* fault! *You* let this happen!"

"Maybe we'd better call a doctor?" Melissa suggested.

He went limp. He fixed his frustrated gaze on Melissa and accused, "They've left me! *You* made them go!"

"You're better off without them," Christian assured. "They've got you into a mess of trouble."

"No!" Steven protested. "No! No! No! No! No!"

They hauled him, chair and all, into the soundproof artisan's room and shut the door behind him.

They waited for the phone call, and Carol looked as if she

would faint when the phone did finally ring. Christian answered and listened to details.

"Someone would like to talk to you, Carol." Christian handed over the receiver.

"John? Oh, John!"

"Is he all right?" Melissa asked Christian who moved beside her, his arm around her waist.

"He's fine."

"I'm coming!" Carol promised and hung up. "He's okay. He loves me. He wants to marry me. Oh . . ."

She threw her arms around Christian. She moved on to Melissa. She headed for the door.

"Tell John we'll see him later!" Christian called after.

Carol stopped and turned suddenly. "Your knife!" She laid it very gently on a work table by the door. Then, she was gone.

Christian called Inspector Dwighton. "He says to wait here."

"I'm not going anywhere." Melissa wrapped her arms around his neck. "I've got everything I could possibly need at the moment, right here, thank you very much."

"We do make a great team, don't you think?" He ran his fingers through her hair and anchored them there as he kissed her long and deep. Only reluctantly, he eventually stopped long enough to say, "Wouldn't it be a shame to break up such a perfect match?"

His next kiss was equally as marvelous, magnificent, enchanting. It took her breath away with a belying gentleness that made her heart beat faster. "Is that a proposal for marriage?"

"It's a proposal for marriage."

"I accept."

He kissed her yet again, and the resulting electricity flushed her skin an attractive pink and made her breath ragged.

Outside the sky over most of British Columbia was cloudy

and grim. A drizzly, damp rain had begun to fall on trees that were quickly rid of it to turn forest soil to oozy mud. But Melissa paid no attention, the weather could have no effect on her present well-being. Because after all, she was very, very deeply in love with someone who loved her equally well, and like all good love stories, they were finally going to live happily ever after.